*The Dani Driscoll Series*

# Hope, Inc.

*by* Loucinda Sullivan

For KJ Sullivan who encouraged, and nurtured my efforts
with unconditional love.

Special thanks to Brian Rush for planting the seed.

*Somewhere, something incredible*
*is waiting to be known.*
*Carl Sagan*

# CHAPTER 1

"Driscoll?"

"Gone home." Dani Driscoll laughed, and peeked around her cubicle to see Editor in Chief, Samuel Cooper, coming her way carrying a fistful of papers.

"I can see that." Coop raised an eyebrow. "I'd like you to take a look at this press release. Can you squeeze it in before the Romano piece?"

"What's it about? Some new-and-improved sports car that perhaps runs on solar?" Dani teased.

Coop rolled his eyes. "No. I think you'll find this more interesting. It's not strictly your beat, but I'd like you to cover it from a human-interest view point."

Dani snatched the papers out of his hand, and rolled her eyes. "This is all scrunched up, Coop. Have some respect for my work." She smoothed the papers on her desk, and read the first few lines out loud. "The Rush Institute, Denver, Colorado. Promising research gives hope to millions."

"You're right, I don't do medical. Pete will be mad. Why me?"

"I want a woman's perspective on this; the story behind the story," Coop told her.

"Great." she said. "But you know I have no background in medical research."

Scanning the next few paragraphs she gasped, and looked up at him with wide eyes.

THE RUSH INSTITUTE

TEN DAYS EARLIER


Dr. Nolan Jennings swiped his security card in the reader, and walked briskly through his lab calling out a happy "Good Morning" on the way to his private office.

His research team was already performing their morning check on the mice, and making notes to enter into the animal trial database. Eager for an update on their findings, he quickly listened to messages, hoping for at least one response to his latest round of grant proposals.

The research had been peer reviewed, and published in the prestigious "Journal of Immunology and Science". This was groundbreaking science, and he was absolutely confident in his findings. But, securing funding to advance this type of research was proving to be difficult. In medicine, the biggest breakthroughs were often met with the most resistance.

*Is the world ready*? He wondered for about the hundredth time. A quick scan of his email revealed nothing urgent, so he pulled on his lab coat and strode into the lab.

"How is everyone this morning? And how are our little ones fairing?"

"Still no evidence of disease." Bridget Mallory leaned over one of the cages, then stood up and removed her glasses, as she did about fifty times a day.

"Excellent! What about the group bred for disease?" Nolan asked.

"None of them have developed a single symptom." Seth McCleary called out from his desk, which was nothing more than a lowered continuation of the black lab counter top with the addition of a few built in drawers and cubbyholes he'd stuffed with mail, notes, and journals. "Any word from the foundation?"

"Not yet. It takes time." Nolan surveyed the wall of cages that housed the mice, and stuck his finger through to pet a few of them.

The door buzzer sounded, and Bridget moved quickly to open it for Amy Garcia, who balanced a tray of coffee, and a box of donuts. Setting the pastries down in the designated break area, she passed out coffee, and took a read of their faces. "No word yet?" She asked in her Texas drawl.

"I'm sure we'll hear soon." Bridget smiled, put her glasses on, and bent over to observe the mice.

Nolan took a sip of his coffee, plopped two donuts on a paper towel, and headed back to his office. "If anyone needs me I'll be up to my nose in another grant proposal."

Amy called after him, "When are we going to sequence your DNA so we can clone your metabolism?"

"It's not genetics, it's gender," Nolan called back.

"It's because you don't sleep," Bridget teased.

Nolan's cell phone rang just as he settled down at his computer. Before he could answer he heard Seth scramble to get out of his chair without falling. Shaking his head, he picked up the call. "Nolan Jennings. Oh yes, Ms. Davenport how are you? Good, good. Uh huh. Yes, a site visit can be arranged at your convenience. Perfect. I'll see you in a few days. Thank you for your consideration. I will, I will. Have a nice day."

"Yes!" Nolan pumped his fist in victory. "We're at the top of the heap! Mona Davenport is coming to our little ol' laboratory. She wants to do a site visit, and she's bringing some members of her advisory board."

All three of them burst into his office high-fiving, Amy jumped up and down, her long dark ponytail bouncing behind her.

"You'll make history, Nolan." Bridget's eyes glistened with tears that hadn't yet spilled over. "In the company of Salk and Pasteur."

"Yes you will." Seth nodded and smiled.

"Our team will make history," Nolan emphasized. "It's always our team. I couldn't have done this without the three of you."

Nolan beamed. His research was finally ready for prime time. Ready to test in human clinical trials, and if it worked in humans the way it worked in mice, it could save millions from a horrible disease.

Nolan buried his head in his hands in mock despair. "If we get funding I'll have another truck load of paperwork to get permission from the FDA to test it."

Amy patted his shoulder. "Awww, there's always a down side, but it's so worth it."

A timer went off in the lab. "Back to work." Bridget shoved on her glasses and headed toward the experiment she'd set up.

"And I need to get this morning's data recorded in the database." Amy turned gracefully on her heels and followed Bridget out the door.

Seth extended his hand to Nolan for their secret handshake, and nodded.

After calling his wife, Suzanne, to tell her the good news, Nolan took two big bites from his donut, and chugged half his coffee.

He never minded publishing and research–those were the gratifying aspects of his work. But, grant proposals also went with the territory, and even after eighteen years as an immunologist Nolan much preferred to be in his lab with his test tubes and mice.

A week after Mona Davenport's team toured the Jennings lab, Nolan shoved an overstuffed binder into the bookcase in his office, and joined his team.

"Is our success rate holding up, Amy?" Nolan asked.

"We can't get better than one hundred percent." She smiled, looking up from her computer. "I'm so excited about our results, I can barely contain myself. But, it makes me sad to think about all the patients who are diagnosed everyday while we wait on funding. I can't believe we haven't heard from Ms. Davenport. The site visit seemed to go so well, and honestly, I expected her to jump on it." Amy shook her head, frowning.

"I know," Bridget said. "She seemed genuinely impressed, and her team was very thorough in their review process. They seemed interested in every detail. I can't think of a more perfect fit for her foundation. But, I did notice that two of the men from her advisory board didn't say much during the tour. They just looked around and scribbled in their notebooks."

"I noticed that, too. Deadpan expressions and no enthusiasm at all." Nolan shrugged and stood with his hands in his lab coat pockets. "Seth, are supplies ordered for the new project? I want it to fall on the heels of this vaccine."

Rocking back precariously in his chair, Seth nodded. "Everything is already stocked, and I have the experiments ready to start Monday morning."

"I'll get that up on the board." Bridget pulled her glasses out of her lab coat pocket, shoved them on her face, and grabbed a marker, writing neatly on the large whiteboard. "Oh, and remember you have that interview with Dani Driscoll from the Denver Tribune on Monday, Nolan."

Nodding, "It's on my calendar. I wouldn't miss it for anything. She's a good reporter; I hope she can get us some publicity. And speaking of things not to be missed, our reservation at Aleandro's is at 7:30 Sunday evening. Everyone still on board?"

"Are you kidding? We wouldn't miss a chance for you to pick up the tab." Seth draped his lab coat over his chair. "I'll walk out with you."


SUNDAY EVENING

ALEANDRO'S RESTAURANT


Seth stood up, and raised his champagne glass. "To Nolan, whose research is on the brink of saving millions of lives every single year."

"To Nolan." Amy, Bridget, and Suzanne said in unison, and clinked their champagne flutes with Nolan's.

"Suzanne, you must be so proud of your husband." Bridget said. "I can't help but notice the admiration in your eyes. It lights up your whole face."

Susanne nodded. "I couldn't be prouder. And Nolan insists the three of you are equally responsible for the success of his research."

"Not true," Amy said. "Nolan is our fearless leader, and we are merely minions doing his bidding."

"Look!" Seth pointed at Nolan. "His head is getting bigger by the minute. You girls better knock it off with the compliments or his enormous ego won't fit through the door of the lab in the morning."

"Seth!" Amy punched him on the shoulder.

The steak and lobster were mouthwatering. But Seth could hardly take his eyes off Amy the entire evening. That little black dress, those long legs even sexier in stilettos, hair flowing like silk over smooth shoulders. Her southern charm and gentle way came out more with each sip of champagne. He found her irresistible tonight.

They celebrated into the evening until Seth noticed Suzanne's eyelids getting heavy.

Nolan reached over, and took her hand. "Ready to call it a night, love?"

Suzanne tried, unsuccessfully, to stifle a yawn. "I guess all the excitement tired me. I hope the rest of you will stay. Nolan will leave his credit card with the waiter."

Seth pushed back from the table. "I'm stuffed and getting tired myself."

Pulling his keys from his pocket, Seth nodded toward his car. "Is everyone okay to drive? I switched to water and coffee awhile ago; I can chauffer all of you."

"I wouldn't mind a ride." Amy seemed grateful for the offer.

"I'm okay, but thanks Seth." Bridget hugged Suzanne, and smiled at Nolan. "Thank you again for a decadent dinner." Waving, she headed to her car. "Have a nice evening, everyone. I'll see you all in the morning bright and early."

Seth chuckled, and watched as Nolan took Suzanne's hand, waved at his colleagues, and started across the street.

"Nolan!" Suzanne shouted, and Seth turned just in time to see the see an old Cadillac sedan slam into Nolan's back with a sickening crack, sending him soaring.

Nolan felt his wife jerk his arm, but the force ripped him away from her. In an instant he was in the air. Higher, higher...

Dizzy and confused, he looked down and saw Suzanne's eyes wide, her mouth open in a piercing scream. "*No-lannnn...*"

*Can't breathe!* Panic gripped him. Pain seared his spine. The impact knocked the air from his lungs, and everything went into slow motion. He could hear Suzanne crying out for him in the street below. The pain of a thousand tiny razors coursed fiercely through his body.

He gasped for air, arms and legs flailing. His heart raced with panic when he realized the black pavement was rushing toward him. He could see all of them; hear their shouts, and then... Nothing.

"Nolan!" Suzanne screamed.

Seth rushed to keep her from running into the street, quickly looking over his shoulder to see if Amy and Bridget were safe. He whipped around in time to see the sedan speeding away into the night; horrified that he never saw its brake lights come on.

"Oh, my God, stop!" Seth screamed after the car.

Nolan crashed to the street with the horrific sound of shattering bones.

"Call 911!" Bridget shouted. She struggled with her purse to find her cell phone.

Amy sank to her knees on the sidewalk. "Oh, please, please, somebody *help* us! We need an ambulance!"

Seth was in the street, at Nolan's side in an instant.

The angle of Nolan's body was frightening. His left leg and foot were twisted and mangled, left arm bent at his side, and right arm lay lifeless above his head. Blood saturated the pant legs of his suit and trickled onto the street, but most alarming was the growing puddle of blood oozing from the back of his head.

Suzanne crumpled beside Nolan, wailing hysterically.

Seth took off his suit jacket and draped it around her, but she ripped it off, reaching out to place it under Nolan's head.

"No, Suz, don't move him until the paramedics get here." He took the jacket from her and draped it around her shoulders again, crouching over to warm her.

She trembled so violently it shook the two of them.

He shouted toward the restaurant, "Has anyone called an ambulance! We need an ambulance here *now*!"

Chaos erupted as customers and employees rushed out of nearby shops and restaurants. Some on their cell phones, some huddled back, and others rushed forward, craning their necks to see.

The blare of the sirens grew louder. Blue, red, and white strobes cut through the night.

Paramedics jumped out of an ambulance carrying large medical kits. One of them ran toward Nolan's unmoving body, pushing a stretcher.

Two Denver police cars screamed in from opposite directions. An officer quickly contained the scene while another handed out clipboards to witnesses, and instructed them to record everything they'd seen.

A woman crossed the street, walking briskly toward the policemen.

Seth heard her recounting what he himself had noticed.

"It all happened so fast," she told them. "And that car… It didn't… It didn't even attempt to stop."

"Write it down on this form." One of the policemen instructed her, handing her a clipboard. "Include as much detail as you can remember, no matter how insignificant it seems."

The police radioed in a hit and run, and took initial statements from Seth, Bridget, and Amy.

Suzanne was pale. She trembled and stared at Nolan, but she didn't speak.

Seth gave the officers Nolan's home address and phone number, and asked if they could contact her later.

"We'll be in touch, but it's important that we get her statement on record now, while the details are fresh."

The policeman turned to Suzanne. "Mrs. Jennings?" He attempted to hand over a pen and clipboard, but she only looked at him. "This will help us find the person who hit your husband."

Her eyes looked like watery glass. She'd stopped crying when the ambulance arrived, and hadn't said another word.

Seth put his hands firmly on her shoulders. "Suzanne, are you okay?"

One of the paramedics hurried over and wrapped a blanket around her. "Ma'am, are you all right?"

She clutched at her chest, and stood swaying. Her wide-eyes darted from the paramedic, to the policeman, to Seth, and back to Nolan.

Seth took her in his arms while paramedics loaded her husband into the ambulance. She pushed free and tried to climb into the back of the ambulance with her husband.

"Ma'am you can go with us, but you'll have to ride up front."

Seth helped her into the passenger side, fastened her seatbelt for her, and closed the door. Looking into her frantic eyes, he yelled after her just before the ambulance turned on the lights, and pulled away. "We'll be right behind you, Suzanne. We'll meet you at the hospital, do you understand?"

The ambulance drove off with a police car following close behind, its sirens blaring.

Seth turned to find Amy sitting on the curb sobbing with her face in her hands. Bridget sat beside her, hands shaking as she wiped blood off her shoes with a tissue.

He reached down, took their hands, pulled them to their feet, and hugged them both tightly. "The police have our information, and they'll be in touch. I'll drive, let's go."

Humming the theme from Mission Impossible, a smirk spread across his face when a police car passed him, lights pulsing through the night. Snipes looked in the rear-view mirror when he heard another siren, and saw an ambulance turning onto the street behind him, heading in the opposite direction.

Pounding the steering wheel to the tune in his head, he drove across town, and turned into a gravel alley lined with rotting fences and filthy trashcans. He pulled into a dirt driveway, got out, heaved open the door to a dilapidated garage, and pulled the car in slowly. It was a tight fit for the '71 Coup Deville but he managed just fine, and patted it fondly when he got out to assess the damage. *Not bad–blends right in with the other scrapes and dents.*

Snipes rummaged through some boxes, and found a rag and a can of gasoline. He wiped down the front end, looking closely for blood, but it was hard to see blood on the dull black surface. *I'll run it through the car wash in the morning, just in case.*

The screen door slammed behind him when he let himself through the back door of the tiny, ramshackle house he rented month-to-month. After tossing his well-worn denim jacket over a chair, and washing the gasoline from his hands at the kitchen sink, he opened a can of beer, drank it down standing in front of the open refrigerator, and grabbed another one.

Flopping down on the threadbare sofa, he pressed the only number programmed into his untraceable cell phone, and waited for an answer. "Done. When can I expect the drop?

Yeah, I hate to get rid of it—it's a classic, but I'll do it as soon as I collect. Later."

# CHAPTER 2

*Send.* Dani logged out of the secure server of the Denver Tribune, closed her laptop, stretched her arms, and yawned. She was working on a series of stories about Colorado's ten most successful women, and had just finished a piece about the owner of the biggest independent real estate company in the state.

*After midnight.* Yawning again, she pattered barefoot in the dark to the kitchen, grabbed a yogurt from the refrigerator, and stood at the sink spooning dinner from the plastic cup.

She found her husband sound asleep, so she slipped out of her clothes, and quietly into bed, snuggling close when he turned over to spoon her.

"Story filed, sweetheart?" Charles asked.

"Five minutes ago. I didn't mean to wake you, though. Have I told you lately you're the world's best husband?"

"Am I now?"

Picking up on his mischievous tone, she turned over to kiss him. "You are," she said, nuzzling his neck and breathing him in. "And you smell good too, but I need to sleep." She leaned up on one elbow, and planted a kiss on his cheek with a twinge of guilt tugging at her heartstrings. "Night-night."

The radio blasted the familiar talk show that woke her at six every morning with lively, sometimes-controversial conversation, interspersed with upbeat music. The ritual got her mind and body in gear, and she bounced down the stairs to the tune of "I Love Rock and Roll" by Joan Jett and the Blackhearts.

She put on a pot of coffee and sipped a glass of water, watching the birds flitting around the Colorado blue spruce outside the kitchen window. A breeze blew gently through the grove of aspen trees, still green in the crisp morning air of September.

She and Charles had sacrificed a few upper cabinets for a wall of windows when they renovated the kitchen but the view of mature trees and flower gardens never failed to make her smile.

Dani showered while the coffee brewed. She grabbed a towel, patted dry, and slathered on her favorite all natural lotion. She pulled on a cotton terry robe, and toweled her razored crop of dark brown hair, deciding this would be a good weekend to stay home cuddled up with her husband.

Charles came in with two cups of steaming black coffee, and handed her one.

"Thank you." She smiled up at him, bringing her favorite Italian mug to her nose, breathing in the rich aroma. "There is nothing better than the first cup of coffee in the morning, is there?"

He grinned down at her. "I can think of at least one." Slipping off his boxers seductively without taking his eyes off hers, he tugged at her hand, leaning toward the shower. "Care to join me?"

Charles was gorgeous in a bad-boy sort of way. Dark waves of hair framed his softly chiseled face, and high cheekbones were compliments of a distant Native American relative. His hazel eyes brooded mysteriously when his mood changed, and intensified when he wore blue, making them even more gorgeous. Volumes hid deep within those eyes, and more than once she'd wished she were an artist, so she could capture his face on canvas.

She giggled and pulled away. "Tempting, but I have a staff meeting and no time for a second shower. Do you have any plans for the weekend?" She ran a comb through her wet hair and fluffed it up with her fingers.

"Not really," he said. "I could work on some loan apps, but they can wait 'til Monday. What do you have in mind?"

"Snuggling." She smiled at him. "A nice bottle of wine, some time to de-stress together, maybe a walk in the park?"

"Sex!" Charles said, pulling her close. He looked at her with the mischievous grin that had captured her heart six years ago. "Lots of sex."

"Yes," she giggled, "lots of sex." She took his face in her hands and kissed him. "You're such a distraction when you're naked. Get in the shower so I can make it out of the house un-jumped."

# CHAPTER 3

Dani closed her copy of the Journal of Science and Immunology, tucked it into her satchel, and rubbed her face. *I'm sure glad Pete has the medical beat.*

At precisely ten a.m., she checked in at the security desk at The Rush Institute and waited for an escort to the Jennings Lab. Ten minutes later she noticed a disheveled-looking young woman stop briefly at the security desk, whisper to the guards, and nod. Dani was surprised to see the woman turn and head to the waiting area to greet her.

"Miss Driscoll, I'm terribly sorry to keep you waiting. I'm Bridget Mallory, one of Dr. Jennings' researchers. Let's borrow this conference room for a moment."

She followed Bridget down a short hallway, and waited while the woman swiped her security card in the door with a trembling hand. "Please sit down. I don't know how to say this."

Dani could see that Bridget was distressed. "He's running late? No worries at all, it happens all the time. I don't mind waiting." Dani made an effort to keep her voice pleasant and soothing. She could tell there was more; Bridget was clearly choking back tears.

"Miss Mallory, what's wrong?"

"Nolan... Dr. Jennings had an accident last night." Her voice quivered. "We were... He was..." She choked back a sob and took in a deep breath. "He's in the hospital. In intensive care, and not doing very well at all." Bridget's voice broke and a stream of tears spilled down her cheek.

*I can't believe I didn't pick up a newspaper this morning.* Dani reached for the box of tissues sitting in the middle of the table, and handed several to Bridget. "I'm so sorry to hear about Dr. Jennings' accident. This must be very hard for you. Have you worked with him for a long time?" Dani laid her hand gently over Bridget's.

She nodded, and responded with a shaking voice. "It's the most rewarding job I've ever had." Tears streamed down her face now. "I've been with Nolan for almost nine years. He's a brilliant researcher, and our recent findings... His research is such a wonderful gift to the world. More than anything, I want him to live to see this vaccine approved, and breast cancer prevented the same way measles and HPV have been. Now I don't know what will happen."

Bridget's shoulders shook, and she buried her face in the handful of tissues, sobbing. When she regained her composure she looked at Dani with sad eyes. "I don't know what will happen to Nolan, or what the future holds for our research."

The woman looked shattered. What in the world had happened? "Bridget, can I get you something? Water? Coffee? A sandwich?"

Bridget mopped her face, and took a shaky breath. "No thank you, Miss Driscoll. I'm sorry about the outburst. You had an appointment, and I didn't think to call you this morning."

"I'm sure you've been more than a little distracted. Please don't worry at all about me," Dani said.

"I can still show you the lab, if you'd like to see it." My colleagues, Seth and Amy, are upstairs. We were given the day off, but we needed to check on the mice."

"Yes, I would like to see the lab if you feel up to it."

"It will help if we stay busy." Bridget said.


Dani drove back to the Trib and restlessly paged through her notes, trying to find an angle on the story that had taken a precipitous turn from hope, and veered toward tragedy. This was definitely not her style of reporting. She stood up, paced for a minute, then headed to the editor's office.

"Coop? Did you know Dr. Jennings was hit by a car last night, and he's in the hospital?"

Coop looked up from the computer, waved her in, and held up a finger, signaling her to wait while he tabbed through the stories filed since the morning edition went to press. "Jason covered an accident over by Aleandro's last night. It was too late to make today's edition, but it's on the website. Let me see… Yes, a hit and run. Dr. Nolan Jennings."

"Needless to say, I didn't get the interview I went for. His colleagues were kind enough to show me around the lab, but they're devastated. They're keeping things running in the absence of Dr. Jennings, but expressed deep concern about his condition. Apparently it's serious. He's in a coma. What do you want me to do with this story now?"

"Write it up, Driscoll. Write it from the perspective of the initial press release, turned tragedy. Then get over to the hospital and see what you can dig up for a follow-up piece to both the hit and run, and the research."

"Well, I can craft the vaccine into a human interest piece, but a follow-up? Shouldn't Pete or Jason…"

"Driscoll, I know what you're capable of. Pour your heart into this piece, and the readers will eat it up. Hope for millions of women is teetering on the life of Dr. Nolan Jennings. This is front page news now."

Dani filed her story then drove to the hospital, even though she knew she couldn't interview a comatose patient. She realized the hospital was prohibited from releasing any information, but maybe she could find a family member, or friend.

Walking out of the elevator on the sixth floor, she scanned the faces of the dozen or so people waiting in the hospitality room for Intensive Care. "Is Suzanne Jennings here?"

Several of them looked up at her with disinterest, and went back to thumbing through magazines, reading books, and sipping coffee or soft drinks.

Dani found an empty chair beside a man wearing a tailored suit, reading the Denver Tribune. She didn't see the cup of coffee sitting on the floor, and knocked it over with her foot when she sat down. "Oh, excuse me. I'm sorry, can I get you another cup?"

Before he could answer, the door from ICU opened and three women emerged, huddled together, crying. Dani recognized the Jennings family from the photos she'd seen earlier in Dr. Jennings' office, and approached them, but the youngest woman stared her down.

Dani turned directly to Suzanne, "Mrs. Jennings? I'm Dani Driscoll from the Denver Tribune."

"Oh my God, not now!" The young woman struggled to support her mother while keeping Dani at bay. "My father just died!"

Suzanne walked toward a line of chairs on shaky legs. "Girls, I need to sit down for a moment."

Several people in the waiting area looked up sympathetically, and the man who'd been reading a newspaper folded it up, and walked briskly to the elevators. Dani got three bottles of water from the vending machine, handed them to the Jennings family, and quietly took a seat on the opposite side of the room.

After about twenty minutes, Suzanne spoke quietly, "I'm ready to go home now."

Supported by her daughters, Suzanne reached down, and took Dani's hand. "Thank you for coming, dear. Nolan would have liked meeting you."

The gentle kindness of Suzanne Jennings, even in grief, nearly ripped Dani's heart out. She called Coop from the parking lot and gave him the news of Nolan's death. "Write it up and send it over as soon as possible. It'll run in the morning edition. You okay, Driscoll?"

"Yeah, but you can tell Pete he can keep his medical beat, I'll stick with my fluff, as he calls it."

# CHAPTER 4

The staff meeting went as expected with stories pitched, discussed, evaluated, and ultimately approved or disapproved by the Editor in Chief, known in his reporter days as Coop the Scoop.

Coop had been a friend of Dani's father's since the two of them attended college at the University of Colorado in Boulder. When Dani survived the accident that claimed both her parents during her sophomore year in college, Coop was the one who comforted and took care of her until her fractured knee, and shattered heart, mended enough for her to return to school.

When he offered an internship at the Denver Tribune she'd been reluctant to work for him. He was like a second father to her, and she was afraid it would be awkward. But, she had hoped to stay in Colorado, and The Trib was simply the best publication for her. She'd interned here, worked as a stringer here, and in the end secured a full time position focusing on business and human-interest stories.

Anxious to shake off the tragedy of her last assignment, Dani began researching Honey Romano. She sat at her desk, rubbing the knee that reminded her of the accident every time it ached. It seemed her knee and her heart would be forever connected.

Nearly everyone in Colorado recognized Honey. Her claim to fame was not only due to the success of her fleet of dealerships—twenty and counting—you couldn't turn on a local TV station or pick up a newspaper or local magazine without seeing Honey featured in an ad with her slogan, "Get a Honey of a Deal," prominently displayed.

By nature of promoting her business Honey was a public figure, and Dani wanted to write more about her than the fact that she had grown a one-dealership family business into the most respected automobile dealerships in the state. Her readers would also want to know about Honey the woman, wife, and mother.

Deciding her aching knee would feel better if she moved around a bit, Dani organized some last notes for the interview, grabbed her keys and steno pad, and drove to Romano Chevrolet to chat with the staff. *Maybe I can gain some insight for the article while I get my oil changed.*

The staff doted on Honey without exception. They spoke of her dedication to the business and of her interest in their own personal successes. They felt they had better than industry-average employee benefits and appreciated Romano Motors' willingness to be flexible with their personal schedules and career goals.

Still curious, Dani drove to Romano Buick-Cadillac, and gathered similar comments from Honey's staff. They remarked on her commitment to customer satisfaction while always backing up the integrity of her employees. No small accomplishment in a business as big as hers.

On Friday morning Dani pulled on a pair of designer jeans, a bright, tailored jacket, and her favorite ankle boots. After almost ten years of writing this type of story she was looking forward to her interview with Honey.

She pulled into Romano Imports, taking note of the opulent sports cars strategically parked around the lot to showcase each one with plenty of room to walk around and admire them. *An extravagant use of expensive real estate*, she thought.

She had driven past this dealership many times, but had never taken the time to stop and browse. And why should she? These cars were priced into the stratosphere, as far as she was concerned. "Impressive," she said under her breath.

She got out of her car and waved at Tribune photographer, James Lathum, who was busy snapping photos of a baby blue Aston Martin Vanquish, obviously in his photo-artistic zone.

Honey walked out of the front doors of the showroom at a confident clip, her arm outstretched to greet Dani with a handshake. Trim and gorgeous in a navy blue pantsuit, gleaming platinum jewelry, blonde hair bouncing past her shoulders, she seemed much younger than her forty-three years. Though small in stature at just over five feet, she definitely commanded attention.

James took a break from photographing the Vanquish, and came over to snap a few of their greeting.

"You're such a guy." Dani teased him when he leaned toward the car before following them inside.

Honey led them upstairs to her private office, which overlooked the showroom behind a wall of glass. The office was furnished with contemporary pieces, and Honey motioned them toward a large glass conference table flanked by red leather Herman Miller chairs. A large family portrait hung above Honey's L-shaped walnut desk, and framed photos of her little girls were placed tastefully around the office.

A secretary brought in a tray of coffee and biscotti, and asked if they required anything more.

James visually swept the room, dumped his camera gear out of photo range, and continued snapping photos of Honey.

*There's probably not a bad photo of her anywhere,* Dani thought.

Honey explained that her father had bequeathed Romano Imports to her when he retired twelve years ago. "I practically grew up here," she said. "I was here every day after school, and on weekends. My dad used to let me sweep the lot and keep any loose change I found. This place is so full of family memories it's inseparable from my private life."

"The lot is impressive, Honey." Dani poised her pen over her notebook. "How did you arrive at the decision to expand after all those years as a single, and very exclusive, dealership?"

"My love of family, cars, and people are the reasons I decided to add Romano Buick-Cadillac." Honey turned her palms up. "Not everyone can afford a Maserati or a Porsche." She broke off a piece of biscotti and dunked it in her coffee. "It went so well I progressively grew the business to add Chevrolet, Ford, and Jeep."

"What do you like most about your business?"

Honey flashed her million-dollar smile. "I enjoy watching the dynamic between car and personality. I love matching cars with the customers who come on our lots. It's a little game I play. I never give the customer my opinion and I manage to guess which car they'll choose about ninety-nine percent of the time. After chatting with a customer for about five minutes I know, right down to the color they prefer. My favorite car is always the one they're buying and it's not purely salesmanship since I don't offer brands I wouldn't drive myself, or put my little girls in."

"How do you keep up with a business spread out across the entire state?"

"At least one day a week I work one of the lots. I hand off my sales to either the newest sales person, or one who is having an off month. It gives them a confidence boost, and it keeps me in touch with my business."

Dani nodded. "That explains why your employees seem to love you. Romano Motors seems to have unusually high employee satisfaction."

Honey responded by saying she has laser sharp intuition about people. "I know the right person when I interview, and I've had a hand in hiring almost everyone who works for Romano. We are family. One enormous family wrapped up in a car business. I'm fond of all of them. If I had to give just one reason for the success of Romano Motors, I would attribute it to our staff."

The interview was moving along nicely since Honey was so open and sincere about her growing business. Dani scanned her notes, shifted in her chair, and looked directly into Honey's deep blue eyes.

"I'd like to change the subject to another success you've had, Honey. You had a brush with breast cancer a couple of years ago, and today you're positively glowing. I'd like to ask you about that time, if you don't mind."

Honey stiffened. "I did have breast cancer, but I don't typically talk about it, especially to the press.

"May I ask why, Honey? I did some research on it for another article recently, and it affects women in staggering numbers."

Honey let out a slow breath, and nodded. "Yes, I'm aware of the statistics, and frankly they scare me. My daughters are at risk. And I've done enough reading on the subject to know that you're at risk too, Dani. Every woman is. And, men aren't immune to breast cancer, either. I haven't discussed it publically because I don't want to be remembered for my cancer. That's not the legacy I want to leave for my children."

"I hadn't thought about it that way." Dani thought it was all she was getting, but Honey sat back in her chair, folded her hands, and continued.

"I read your article about the research at The Rush Institute. I was heartbroken to hear Dr. Jennings died so tragically."

"Yes, it's very sad. I met his staff the morning after the accident. They're devastated."

"Do you know what will happen to his research now?"

"No one knows yet," Dani said. "The researchers on his staff said Rush hasn't made a decision, but the grants are funded in Dr. Jennings' name, and that's a problem until they figure it out. Apparently, they'll need to reapply for funding under the name of a new principal investigator if they want to proceed with the vaccine."

"That research is the most promising I've heard. Prevention is desperately needed." Honey said.

Dani detected sadness behind Honey's smile, so she continued carefully. "There does seem to be an endless stream of research being conducted. Are you planning to get involved with one of the breast cancer charities now?"

Honey's lips quivered; her tone was defiant. "No. I have no interest in being a part of leading lambs to slaughter."

Dani set her pen and notepad on the desk and studied Honey's face. "I can see this is an emotional subject for you, Honey. I'm sorry if I made you feel uncomfortable, but I don't understand what you mean. Lambs to slaughter?"

Honey continued, "Don't misunderstand me. I care deeply about preventing breast cancer. But none of the charities that came to me for support spend a satisfactory percentage of donations on research for prevention. In fact, the majority of them don't fund prevention at all."

Honey leaned forward and folded her hands on her desk. "Let me share something with you, Dani. When I was diagnosed, one of the first things I did was join the discussions on my social networks. The women participating in those threads are my heroines. They were in various stages treatment and survival themselves, yet they were open and willing to share their experiences with anyone who might benefit. No matter what question I asked, someone was willing to jump in and help. They bared their souls for me, and I'll never forget them."

"That's lovely, Honey. But, then why are you so opposed to the charities?" Dani grabbed her steno pad.

"I honestly planned to support Mona Davenport's organization, since she's local. But, as a businesswoman, I always do my homework. What I found was appalling, so I looked into some others. The balance sheets I looked at prove most of these organizations spend a disproportionate percentage of donations on overhead, salaries, and awareness. I believe most women are aware of breast cancer already, so in my opinion those campaigns are nothing more than a form of self-promotion. A very small percentage of the money raised is spent on research. That explains why over three decades, the incidence of breast cancer has actually increased by twenty-three percent. Some of these charitable foundations have become adept at creating and promoting an illusion."

"I had no idea." Dani took notes.

"They raise millions every year based on the promise of a cure because prevention would put most of them out of business, wouldn't it? They're using semantics to create a ruse. They say cure and a lot of women believe that includes prevention. It's not the same thing. I want prevention for my daughters, not the so-called cures I endured for almost a year."

"I had no idea you felt so strongly about this." Dani said.

"I'm passionate about finding the right research to get behind. The Jennings vaccine offered hope of prevention. His death was an enormous setback for women."

Honey said up straight and adjusted her jacket. "For now, I'm happy to have survived the treatments and the cancer. I pray every day I can stay healthy so I can raise my girls."

"I hope so too, Honey." Dani nodded and, preferring to end the interview on a happy note, she changed the subject. "Will you show us the car you drive?"

"I'd love to." Her beautiful smile returned and she sprang from her chair. "I drive two, but I'll show you the one I drove today."

A gleaming convertible Bentley Continental GTC in Special Magnolia Pearlescent was parked in a private spot. James asked her to pose inside, then outside the car, as she chatted easily again.

"I drive this one to the office most of the time. On snowy days, and when I have my girls with me, I drive a Jeep

Grand Cherokee Limited. I love the color of my Jeep. It's called Winter Chill."

"Would it be possible to get a photo of you and your girls with the Jeep?" James chimed in.

"Sure. Tomorrow is Saturday. Why don't we meet here at 11:00?"

She noted the time on her cell phone and remembered her plans to relax with Charles for the weekend. Snapping a few photos shouldn't take long, and it would add dimension to the story. Charles would tease her, but he'd understand.

Dani waved at a neighbor jogging past her yard pushing a baby stroller, and pulled up to her Craftsman-style home.

She loved living in Washington Park. It was one of Denver's oldest neighborhoods, and represented everything she loved about the city. Residents walked to charming boutiques, restaurants, and coffee shops that had sprung up around the extensive neighborhood. Families wandered around lakes and enjoyed community activities in the park.

An eclectic mix of late 19th century bungalows were interspersed with large stately homes, some of which had been torn down in favor of newer construction. To Dani, Wash Park represented the epitome of America. It was a melting pot of homes, and the people who lived in them.

Charles was pouring a glass of Chianti when she walked in. "Happy Friday. Chicken is marinating in the fridge."

"Thank you for doing that. It has been a happy Friday. How was your day?" Dani asked.

He handed her a glass of wine. "My day was good. We took on a new client. It's a software startup with an interesting angle. The guys who started the company have extensive experience and submitted a well-documented loan package earlier in the week. I called them just before I left the bank and told them their loan is approved. It was a nice way to end my week, and I'm sure it made their weekend."

"To your successful week." Dani clinked her glass against his.

Charles led her by the hand to the swing on the covered front porch.

She relaxed and rocked the swing gently. "You would have loved the cars I saw today at Romano Imports."

"Aw, Sweetheart you don't need to shop for expensive toys to get my attention." He winked at her.

"I was thinking you might like to go with me tomorrow and browse around. There are some magnificent cars on that lot."

"I'm sure that's true, but not in our price range." He raised an eyebrow. "Do I detect an underlying motive?"

Dani lowered her head in mock shame, grinned, and looked at him batting her eyelashes. "Just for an hour or so. It

38

wouldn't look right if I didn't show. We can still sleep late, and afterward we can go somewhere for a leisurely lunch."

"All right," he teased. "But don't complain to me about car payments if I drive off the lot in a Lamborghini."

Seven year-old Katie and four year-old Olivia hammed it up for the camera and Dani pretended to interview them.

"Your adorable daughters will add a personal dynamic to the story."

"They're what I'm most proud of." Honey beamed.

Dani looked around the lot for Charles, who was keeping himself occupied with a chocolate Porsche 911 Cabriolet convertible. When James was finished with his photos Honey sent the girls inside and strolled across the lot with Dani to greet him.

"This Cabriolet is perfect for you. I can offer you a great deal on it. It's a trade-in from a customer who buys a new Porsche every year."

"It looks brand new." Charles slid into the drivers seat and admired the dash, stroked the leather passenger seat, and tried his hand on the gearshift. "I'm not really in the market for a car, though I must admit this one is impressive."

Dani grinned. "In this case, the driver brings the wow-factor. It suits you, Charles."

"You know, we're closed tomorrow," Honey said. "Why don't you take the car for the weekend? Consider it a thank you for sharing Dani with us this morning."

Dani's mouth flew open. "Oh Charles, say yes. I'll pack a picnic and we'll drive up to Estes Park." She waved her arm at the sky. "It's a beautiful day for a drive."

Charles rolled his eyes and grinned at her. "I don't know which is more irresistible, you or the car."

He turned to Honey. "I would love to borrow the car, if you're sure."

"It would be my pleasure."

Dani hopped up and down with her iPhone, shooting photos of Charles sitting in the Porsche while they waited for Honey to get a dealer plate and some paperwork.

"Aren't you glad you tagged along with me this morning?" She grinned at him.

Charles grinned back and blew her a kiss.


The drive northwest into Estes Park was gorgeous in September. Dani rested her head on the seat of the convertible, basking in the sun with the wind whipping through her hair.

She peeked over at Charles, who was clearly enjoying the power of the Porsche on the winding roads.

The scenery changed from hillsides to forest lined roads, revealing occasional glimpses of the Rocky Mountains.

"Oh, this is one of my favorite parts of the drive," she said. They crested a hill, and the splendor of Lake Estes, dotted with sailboats, unfolded below them.

Dani grabbed the blanket and Charles carried their picnic basket to spot at the lake with a view of the Stanley Hotel on a mountainside in the background.

"Mmmmm. The air smells so fresh up here." Dani sipped the beer Charles had opened for her.

They chatted easily, enjoyed deli sandwiches, and watched colorful sailboats glide across the lake in the breeze. Holding hands, they explored the shops downtown and talked about Honey's generosity.

"Every one of the employees I spoke with mentioned her kindness."

"It seems she's living a charmed life." Charles said.

"Well, I wouldn't exactly say that. Did you know she had breast cancer three years ago?"

Charles shook his head. "I didn't know. She appears to be healthy now. Is she okay?"

"As far as I know she's cancer free, but it's an emotional subject for her."

"Well, I imagine fighting breast cancer feels pretty personal. I'm not sure I'd want to discuss it with the press, if I were in her shoes." Charles said.

"True, but she's been so openly philanthropic over the years I thought she'd add a cancer charity, that's all. She did read my articles about Dr. Jennings and his research at Rush, and is impressed with the new direction he was taking. She pointed out the difference between cure and prevention. I always assumed these charities were behind prevention, but Honey was quick to note that most are raising money for cures, meaning more drugs to treat cancer after it's already diagnosed."

"I never really thought about the difference," Charles said.

"Honey has. And, she's terrified her daughters will have to go through the treatments she went through. It's too bad Dr. Jennings died. An endorsement from Honey would have gone a long way in promoting his preventive research."

Dani pondered quietly for a moment. "She's smart, Charles. I have even more respect for her after that interview."

# CHAPTER 5

"That meddling bitch!" Mona Davenport ripped the article from the newspaper, tipping over a full cup of coffee in the process. Seething, she balled up the article and threw it at the puddle of coffee spreading over her desk.

"Jackie! Get in here and clean up this mess!"

Jackie Tanner rushed through the door to Mona's office, and sprang into action. After tossing the sopping newspaper into the recycle bin, she dashed out the door, calling over her shoulder, "Be right back with a roll of paper towels."

After mopping up the coffee, and setting things right on Mona's desk, she asked, "Mona, what's wrong? What can I do?"

Fingering the diamond broach she wore every day, Mona looked out of the fifteenth story window at the Denver skyline. She'd read Dani's earlier article about Dr. Jennings, but was certain his demise also meant the end of the vaccine. *How could I have been so foolish?*

She adjusted her jacket, gathered her composure, and smiled at her personal assistant. "My apologies, Jackie. I made an error, that's all. It's nothing that can't be remedied. Everything will be fine."

"Do you want me to run down to the lobby and get you another coffee and newspaper?"

"No. No, I've read all the news I care to read today. Cancel this afternoon's staff meeting, will you? There are some things I need to do."


Dani's stomach was growling. Between email, and phone calls she could hardly get to her assignments. *At least I know I'm being read.*

She reached for the phone again. "Dani Driscoll. Oh, Mona, hi. I was hoping to reach you today. Yes, very sad. I was at the hospital when his family got the news. Lunch?" Dani glanced at the clock on her computer. "Sure, one o'clock sounds perfect. I'll meet you there."


Dani was about half a block away when she spotted Mona pacing and talking on her cell phone in front of Los Cabos on the Sixteenth Street Pedestrian Mall.

Mona was a busy woman who had grown her home-office breast cancer charity into a well-run fund raising machine, with branches in every capitol city in the country. Anyone who hadn't heard of the American Pink Ribbon Foundation had to be living on another planet.

Mona reached over and squeezed Dani's hand, then finished her phone call. Looking beautiful and confident, Mona was dressed to the nines in a tailored, cream colored pantsuit, and stunning trademark broach—which an earlier interview had revealed was a custom piece created from the diamonds in her mother's wedding rings designed into the pink ribbon symbol of her foundation.

"Dani dear, thank you for meeting me on such short notice." Mona said.

"My pleasure. You were on my list to call for a follow up on the Jennings research. Let's get a table. I missed breakfast, and I'm running on coffee."

Mona took the menu from the waiter, and turned sympathetically to Dani. "I read your articles on poor Dr. Jennings and wanted to extend my sympathy, dear. I didn't realize you took on those kinds of assignments. That couldn't have been easy for you. Why on earth did Coop send you to cover such a tragedy? It isn't your style at all."

Dani nodded. "You're right. It's definitely not my usual beat, and for that I'm grateful. I'm sure you understand more

of the science behind the research than I do, considering all
the grant proposals you must receive."

Mona nodded. "We do get quite a large number of
proposals each year. Thank goodness for my advisory board."

"Actually, Coop didn't send me to cover Dr. Jennings
death, he sent me to cover the research–the prevention
aspect. It was coincidental that Dr. Jennings passed away on
the evening of my interview. The timing was just all wrong for
my assignment, but Coop wanted me to stick with the story
when things went awry with Dr. Jennings."

"Oh dear. It must have been awful for you. Your
articles are usually so upbeat, and I've always said you are a
master at covering local business, Dani. So you're finished now
with poor Dr. Jennings' story?"

"No. Actually I planned to call you for your reaction to
the news of his vaccine. I want to do a follow-up story with
you; maybe even a series to follow its progress. Honey
Romano is very interested in prevention, and has high hopes
for the research at Rush. She's ready to make a sizeable
contribution to the research, and I think with some coverage it
could get a lot of support."

Mona cocked her head, put her fork down, and looked
at her directly. "Dani, the research consisted of one published
paper, in one publication, from an unknown researcher. Some
of the top oncologists in the country have been working on a

cure for breast cancer for years, and years. My advisory board did a site visit, and they were not impressed."

"But, the Jennings research is about prevention, not another curative drug. My understanding is that the current treatments are very hard on patients, and they experience side effects that last a lifetime. In fact, Honey Romano told me chemotherapy is so destructive, she can no longer be an organ donor. The mice in Dr. Jennings lab trials have experienced no ill side effects at all. Isn't that amazing?"

"Those drugs you're talking about save lives, dear. It's my life's work to find a cure for the horrible disease that took my mother. You must know that." Mona fingered her broach.

"Yes, but..."

"And Dani, I only say this because you've earned such a good reputation at the paper. Any local business would jump at the chance of being interviewed by you. Your features are fantastic. I hate to see you chasing something that might dampen your success."

Dani crossed her legs and leaned back. "I'm not chasing. I think this would be a great topic for a series of human-interest stories. My readers seem to be curious about this."

"The science behind breast cancer is very complex, dear. I fear your lack of expertise would be obvious to readers. You don't really want to put your good reputation on the line by writing trivial pieces, do you?"

"Trivial?" Dani could feel the blood rushing to her cheeks.

"Isn't it unlikely that an unknown researcher would suddenly come up with something that top research centers around the country–around the world really–have been focused on for decades? And honestly, even if poor Dr. Jennings was on the right track, how could the research possibly continue successfully without its creator?"

"You make a good point Mona, but apparently the Rush Institute plans to continue with the research. Dr. Jennings may be dead, but his team is still in place, and they plan to carry on."

"Why, of course that's the perception they're putting out there. The Rush Institute will milk this until the money stops rolling in. I doubt anything will come of this project because my advisory board believes it to be flawed. I don't have a drop of confidence that it will ever make it past the mice in that lab. Dear, don't you see that continuing to cover this story gives false hope to those who are suffering?"

Dani fell silent and played with her salad. How could she be at a loss for words? She was a journalist for heaven's sake. *Say something!*

"I can see your point of view Mona, and I would never knowingly offer false hope to anyone. But, Honey Romano feels this is what women have been waiting for. And my email account is evidence that readers want to know more about this research."

Mona dabbed the corners of her mouth with the linen napkin. "I'll tell you what, dear; I'll call the lab myself, and I promise to call you exclusively if there is anything worth reporting. This is my area of expertise, and I assure you I'll know newsworthy progress when I see it."

Mona insisted on picking up the check, and by the time Dani started back toward the Tribune she was wondering who was interviewing whom. She glanced at her notepad, which was practically devoid of notes. Why had she sat there letting Mona fill her with doubt about her own abilities?

Blood rushed to her cheeks and warmed her face. She picked up her pace, even though her heart was already pounding. What had just happened? She was a reporter, for Pete's sake, a damned good reporter. Even if she wasn't on the medical beat, she was capable of doing the research. This was a good story and by damned, she would write it!

Charging through the front doors of the Tribune, she headed straight for Coop's office. *I'm not waiting for the staff meeting; I'm pitching this story right now.*

Coop was on the phone so she stood at the doorway, but she could hear the strain in his voice.

"Of course we appreciate your business. Understood. Yes, perfectly clear." He hung up and pressed his palms to his head.

"Coop, are you all right?"

"Women!" He looked up at her wearily. "What's up Driscoll?"

"Coop, I have an idea, and I just couldn't wait for the staff meeting. Do you have a minute?"

"Yeah, sure, what is it?" He motioned for her to sit down.

"I'd like to do another series. A series of stories about Dr. Jennings' research, and its potential impact on the lives of women. I could go to the cancer center, and interview…"

"No."

"What?" Her eyes opened wide. The firm dismissal was so unlike Coop she couldn't help it, she giggled at his abrupt answer. "Why?"

"Jennings is dead, and so is the story."

She calmed herself. "Okay, I've caught you when you're busy, I'm sorry. I'll make my notes, and bring them to the meeting."

"No. Dani, the answer is no. I won't run it."

"Coop! You never dismiss me like this. What's wrong?"

Coop was obviously rattled. "Close the door and sit down. This is strictly off the record, do you understand, Driscoll?"

She sat down and watched him furiously tapping his pen on the desk—a habit she'd adopted. "What's going on, Coop? Are you okay?"

Coop hesitated before he began. "Dani, you know you're like a daughter to me. You're also one of my best reporters, and I rarely shut you down. But this time… That was Mona on the phone just now."

"Mona Davenport? I just had lunch…"

"Yes, she told me. And she told me about your series in so many words, and she is… Let's call it miffed."

Dani could tell he was measuring his words carefully.

"Miffed?" Her brow furrowed. "Coop, think about this. Why should she care? I even suggested that I would include her in my interviews. It seems to me she should love to have this kind of coverage. Especially now, since she's gearing up for Breast Cancer Awareness Month." Waving her arm at the window, she added, "The whole city will be pink in two weeks!"

He looked down at his desk and let out a long breath. "She threatened to pull all advertising and make a lot of phone calls. Our advertisers aren't a secret. She just needs to pick up a newspaper and start dialing." He rubbed his palms over his forehead again. "She's very well connected, Dani, and we can't afford to loose advertisers in this economy. Newspapers are shutting down all the time. The Washington Post was just sold, for God's sake. The Washington Post!"

Thinking back over her lunch conversation she tried to make sense of this. "I don't understand. What was her reason?"

"She really wasn't clear about why, but she was clear that she won't let "pseudo-science" make a mockery of her life's work. I don't usually yield to this kind of pressure, but she was quite adamant, and you know how much influence she has in this city."

"I know Coop. I'm sorry if I've put you in an awkward position, but this is a newspaper. We report the news. A vaccine that could prevent breast cancer is a big story, Coop. Since when do we let advertisers dictate what we print?"

"Well, that's a complicated question, as you can imagine. I've made my decision on this. It's not up for discussion." Spreading his fingers out on the desk, he pushed himself up. "This conversation never happened. I don't want the other staff to know about this, are we clear?"

Disheartened, Dani responded, "This conversation never happened, Coop."


Charles could tell as soon as she walked through the door that her day had been a rough one. "Why the gloomy look?"

Smiling at him wearily, she tugged his hand, and led him to the kitchen. "Long day. Want some wine?"

"Sure, I'll join you. Want to sit on the porch, and tell me about it?"

Sighing heavily, she grabbed her glass and the bottle, slumping into a chair at the kitchen table. "No, let's sit here and talk. I could use a nice big dose of sanity right about now."

He kissed the top of her head before he sat across from her. "I can be your sanity check, sounding board, your big strong shoulder–whatever you need."

He listened while she described the odd lunch with Mona followed by Coop's rejection of her series concept. "Sweetheart, you have had a rough day. I think it's a hell of a story idea. Did Coop say why he doesn't want to print it? Maybe he'll sleep on it and change his mind."

"I shouldn't tell you this, Charles, but I need to know if I'm over-reacting. It's confidential, okay?"

"Of course. What's wrong?" Charles reached across the table and took her hand.

After Dani told him about her conversation with Coop, Charles was ready to dive in, and defend her right to tell this story. "Frankly, I'm confused, and astounded. I thought Mona wanted to find a cure. I thought that's what all her fundraising was about."

"I know! But, as Honey said, the Rush vaccine is prevention, not a cure. I thought Mona would be all over this with support, but you should have seen the look on her face when I mentioned Honey's interest in the vaccine. In fact, now that I think about it, why is it Honey, and not Mona, who's interested in furthering the research? Honey is in the business of selling cars. Mona is the one who's in the business of funding breast cancer cures. Or in this case, prevention."

"That's true. Sweetheart, are you sure Coop won't get behind your series? Maybe after the dust settles?"

She took a long sip of wine. "I've known Coop my whole life. That door is firmly closed."

# CHAPTER 6

Even though Nolan's team had been given the rest of the week off, Seth got up and came to the lab as usual, knowing the research would be compromised if anything happened to the mice in their absence.

The familiar pungent scent of mice and chemicals filled his nose. Beakers and flasks soaked in cleaning solution, and an unopened box of new supplies sat beside his desk. The lab looked the same, but the void was palpable.

Bridget was already at work feeding the mice in the control group. Her eyes looked puffy from crying. "What will happen now, do you think?" She took off her glasses and placed them gently on the countertop.

"My guess is the Board of Directors will meet and let us know what they've decided. The research is funded under Nolan's direction, which means we'll have to reapply for the funding we already have. We'll also need to re-submit outstanding grant proposals. Maybe they'll appoint one of the other researchers to take over until they can find someone." Seth slumped in his chair, rocking precariously back and forth.

Bridget stared at him. "The same board that gave us the week off? I hope they realize that research like this can't be abandoned for a week. Seth, do you think they comprehend what Nolan has done? What's at stake?"

Amy came through the door, looking pale. "You're right Bridget, there's so much at stake. Nolan's little ones could have died of starvation if we hadn't shown up, and then all his years of effort would be in shambles! Do you think the Board has already given up on Nolan's research?" She covered her face and cried. "I can't believe we'll never see him again."

Bridget hugged her. "I know. I know. I can't believe he's gone."

"I'll talk to them and make them understand," Seth said. "For now, we'll take care of Nolan's little ones. We know the drill. We'll carry on in Nolan's honor while we wait for the decision."

Bridget turned to him. "Thank you Seth. It feels so strange being here knowing he's never walking through that door again. And I can't stop thinking about poor Suzanne. I keep having flashbacks of her crouching over Nolan in the middle of the street. I should call and ask if I can do anything for her."

After requesting a meeting with one of the board members to discuss the future of the lab, Seth was called to attend a special board session. He arrived at the lab early the next morning wearing a tie, and sports coat.

"Wow! Look at you!" Amy walked over to straighten his tie, and turned to Bridget. "Bridget, have you ever seen this lab rat looking so handsome?"

Tucking her glasses into her lab coat, Bridget smiled. "You look nice, Seth. The meeting's at nine? I'm so glad they included you to give input on what we need. This is a big decision, and I hope they won't take too long making up their minds."

"I've been thinking about that. I expect they'll advertise internationally. The Board knows they have us to carry on the day-to-day protocol, so I imagine they'll take their time and find an expert, maybe even an oncologist."

"Globally?" Amy went back to her computer. "That probably means six months to a year before someone is hired and familiar enough with the research make any progress."

"I doubt an oncologist will look at the research the same way," Bridget said. "It's important to get the right person in here, and one thing's for sure; some lucky bastard will get to walk in and reap the rewards of years of Nolan's efforts." She put on her glasses, and bent down to inspect the next group of mice. "It doesn't seem right, does it little ones?"

"No, it doesn't," Seth said. "But Nolan would want someone to see this research through FDA approval. You know the end result was more important to him than notoriety. He just wanted women to have the option of a vaccine."

He paced back and forth. "Do either of you have any requests or questions for me to pose? I'm headed upstairs now. I'm not about to be late."

"Take a deep breath, Seth. You look like you're ready to blast off. How much coffee have you had this morning?"

"Too much, I guess." He grabbed a notepad, and tucked a pen in his pocket.

"Do Nolan proud, that's all I ask." Bridget smiled at him.

"Tell them we need an immunologist, and the sooner, the better." Amy stood up from her computer, and gave him a friendly hug. "You'll do great, Seth."


Two and a half hours later, Seth walked back to the lab looking solemn.

His colleagues looked at each other, put down what they were doing, and hurried to his side. "What happened?" They asked in unison.

Seth shrugged his jacket off, loosened his tie, and sank down in his chair staring at the floor. He took a long drink of water, trying to shake the intensity of the rapid-fire questioning in the meeting. Now it was up to him to break the news of the board's decision.

He looked at them. "I haven't quite wrapped my head around it yet. I hadn't thought, hadn't realized…"

"What is it Seth? They aren't shutting us down, are they?" Bridget asked. "I can't imagine working on another project at this point. Are we fired?"

Amy's eyes widened, her lip quivered, and she whispered, "*Fired*?"

"No, no, we're all safe." His focus snapped back at the word "fired".

"We'll be continuing right here. The Board recognizes how important Nolan's research is for Rush, and they don't want to miss a beat. They appointed me to head the team. Starting immediately."

Amy bounced up and down, flung her arms wide, and wrapped them around his neck. "Oh my gosh! Seth that's wonderful! Congratulations! Isn't this fantastic, Bridget?"

Bridget looked stunned, but she managed a smile. "Yes, wonderful. Congratulations. I… I'll be right back. Ladies room."

Sprinting down the hallway, tears overflowed before Bridget could lock herself into a stall. Sinking back against the door, she tried to sort through the chaos raging in her head.

*Seth is my boss now? Did he plan this? Did he apply for this appointment behind my back?*

This felt like such a betrayal. She never thought in a million years the board would consider selecting one of them to take over what Nolan had begun. *I have seniority, why didn't the board interview me? This should be my opportunity!*

She tried to sort it out quickly, knowing she had to get back to the lab. Why hadn't she thought to apply for the promotion? She looked at her watch, and taking a long hitching breath, let herself out of the stall and looked in the mirror. *Ugh! My nose is as red as Rudolph's.*

She splashed cold water on her face and looked herself straight in the eyes. *What's the matter with you? Seth is your friend. You should be happy for him.*

Smoothing out her lab coat, and shoving her glasses on, Bridget took a slow, calming breath, and hurried back to the lab.

Sitting in his usual spot the next morning, Seth organized his notes. The transition to lead researcher would need to be handled with sensitivity. He could tell Bridget was upset yesterday, and he didn't blame her. Not even he had expected this outcome.

The Jennings residence was still on auto-dial, but he hesitated a moment to gain his composure before calling. "Suzanne, good morning. How are you? I know, us too. The lab doesn't feel right without him." *She still sounds devastated; this isn't going to be easy.*

"I met with board of directors yesterday, and I wanted your input on how to handle Nolan's office–his personal things. Yes, very fast, they felt it was urgent."

Wanting to answer her question as gently as possible, he measured his words. "Well, it was unexpected, but they appointed me. Thank you Suzanne, that means a lot to me. Would you like to come over and get his personal items? Of course I'd be glad to bring them. Is there anything else I can do for you? Okay, I'll see you around six then? Take care of yourself. Bye Suzanne."

Seth sank back in his chair, rubbing his face.

Amy had arrived during the conversation. She scooted behind him and rubbed his shoulders. "We're behind you one hundred percent, Seth. How can I help?"

"Unfortunately it will fall on us to pack up Nolan's personal belongings. Suzanne wants to me bring them over on my way home tonight. I brought a few boxes. Want to help?"

"Sure thing, boss!" She grinned at him, and tugged his arm to pull him up.

"Bridget, do you want to help?" He couldn't afford to loose her at this point. He needed to find some way to make her understand how important she was to this transition, and to him.

"No, it sounds like you've got it handled. I'll continue with Nolan's little ones." She bit her lip. "I mean our little ones." Hitching in a breath, she shoved on her glasses and balled her unruly curls into a scrunchie.

"Okay, Amy and I will handle the office. We're still allotted a grant writing position and we'll need someone experienced in here as soon as possible. Bridget, will you continue with the job description and requisition? I'd like to get that to Human Resources and start the ball rolling today, if possible."

"Of course," she reached for the phone. "I'll answer this; you two carry on."


"Oh, hello Ms. Davenport... Thank you, we miss him terribly. Sure, yes lunch would be nice, but there's something you should know. Seth is the new primary investigator. Would you rather meet with him? As of yesterday, actually. Oh, you're sweet. Lunch would be great, I'll meet you there."

Bridget walked to the office doorway in time to see a brief embrace. *Well that's just perfect! What other surprises does Seth have in store?* "Ahhemmm."

Amy stepped back and grabbed a framed photo and wrapped it in paper.

"Seth, that was Mona Davenport. She wants to meet me for lunch."

"Thank you for handling that, Bridget. Maybe she has good news for us."

He walked over and stood in front of her with his hands in his pockets. "Bridget, I want you to know that I consider you to be a vital member of this team. We are still a team. I'm sorry we lost Nolan; you know he was a good friend to me. And you're right, I am a lucky bastard to walk into this position."

She nodded, pursed her lips, and went back to her desk.

Mona requested a booth with privacy, and instructed the hostess to seat Bridget when she arrived.

"Bridget, dear!" Mona reached over and gave Bridget a brief hug. "I wanted to extend my condolences in person. This must be very hard for you."

"Thank you Ms. Davenport, I appreciate your thoughtfulness."

"Call me Mona, dear. And, tell me how you're doing. So much has happened since my site visit."

"It's been hard on all of us, especially his wife. I still expect to see Nolan when I walk into the lab. He was always so enthusiastic, and optimistic." Her voice was unsteady when she spoke of him. "I'm not sleeping well since the accident. I must look a mess."

"Of course not! You've been through such an ordeal. And now to hear that Seth McCleary has used poor Dr. Jennings' death to bulldoze his way to a promotion. Isn't it just like a man to assume he's superior? Bridget, the board should have appointed you as the new primary investigator." Mona looked at Bridget sympathetically.

"Actually, I don't think Seth asked for the job. The board..."

"Of course he did. You don't really think that the board of directors at the Rush Institute would hand such a prestigious position to someone who hadn't even expressed an interest, do you dear?"

Bridget shrugged her shoulders and sipped some water.

"And you, dear? What will you do now? I'm sure I can find a position for you in my organization."

"Well, I'll stay at Rush, of course. I've made a big investment in this research, it represents almost nine years of my professional life."

"And that back stabbing Seth rushed right in and scooped it up for himself!"

"Mona, I don't really think that Seth..."

Patting Bridget's hand, Mona continued, "I don't want to upset you, dear. Now tell me, how can I help? Is there anything at all I can do for you?"

"Well yes, fund the research so we can move it to the next phase. Testing in human clinical trials is the next step to getting Nolan's breast cancer prevention into the hands of physicians."

"That's out of my hands now. The decision lies with my advisory board. Is there anything else? Anything at all?"

Bridget buttered a piece of French bread. "I don't really know of anything else. Oh! We are looking for an experienced grant writer. You wouldn't happen to know of anyone, would you?"

Mona rubbed a finger over her broach. "Actually, dear let me make a few phone calls and get back to you. I'm happy to help if I can."

# CHAPTER 7

The staff meeting at the Tribune was more chaotic than usual, due to the presidential election in just over a month.

"I have the presidential and VP candidates covered, but I could use some help with the senate debates." Coop looked up from his pile of paper and scribbled notes. "Volunteers? Ah, Driscoll can you manage tomorrow's debate?"

"I'm on it!" Coop's stance on the Rush series still nagged at her, but she was a professional and knew she had to move on.

After the meeting, she decided to take advantage of the gorgeous Fall day and get outside. She grabbed her laptop and walked to the coffee shop on the mall to do some research. Twitter was bursting at the seams with political chatter, and the exploding cost of healthcare dominated the blogs.

Overhearing two women chatting at the next table, she leaned toward them. "Excuse me. I'm Dani Driscoll of the Denver Tribune and I couldn't help overhearing your conversation. Did you say you spent three-hundred thousand dollars on medical care this year?"

"In the past twelve months, yes." The pale woman looked up at her with a welcoming smile.

"Kelly is so brave. She's endured so much this past year, and look at her. She's still smiling." Obviously proud, Kelly's friend squeezed her hand. "I'm Jenna. It's nice to meet you, Dani. I read your articles all the time. Would you like to join us?"

Dani turned her chair around. "I would, yes. I'm covering the senatorial debate tomorrow, and the cost of medical care in this country seems to be a hot topic. Would you mind if I asked you some questions about your experience?"

"Ask away. I don't mind at all. I hardly have an ounce of modesty left after this past year."

Dani smiled. "I'll try to preserve your dignity. Were you in an accident that caused excessive medical expenses?"

"No, actually I had breast cancer. But, as of today I'm officially "N.E.D." No evidence of disease. I just had my one year checkup and we're celebrating." The two friends tapped their coffee cups together, beaming.

"Three-hundred thousand dollars to treat breast cancer? Wow, I had no idea. That's a significant expenditure. May I ask, whether you have insurance?"

"Yes. Thank goodness I have very good insurance, and only had to pay my copays and deductible. But it's still a large financial burden. Over twenty-thousand dollars in my case. The three-hundred thousand I mentioned was billed to my insurance company."

"That's still a large burden," Dani agreed. "What was the biggest part of the cost? Was it for surgery?"

"No. Actually, more than half was for chemo and other drugs. The cost of some of my medicine was outrageous. My chemotherapy drugs averaged thirty-five hundred dollars per infusion, and I had sixteen infusions over twenty weeks. One of my anti-nausea drugs was over a hundred dollars per dose, but it worked very well and thankfully I didn't throw up even once during chemo."

"Congratulations on beating cancer, Kelly. You look amazing. So your treatment was twenty weeks?"

"No, my medical care lasted for almost a year. I had the big three: chemotherapy, mastectomy, and radiation. My treatments were in a different order than most, because I had a more obscure type of cancer called Inflammatory Breast Cancer. There isn't a lump with IBC. Mine started with a just a small red area about the size of my index finger. I had no pain, or indication that something was wrong."

Dani jotted on her steno pad, more for her own benefit than the story. "All this time I thought I was just checking for lumps."

"I did, too." Jenna piped in. "Kelly was lucky to catch it in time. We've learned that by the time IBC is visible it's at least stage III-b, and it's often misdiagnosed. That's terrifying, isn't it?"

Dani nodded. "Yes, it is. It's interesting that with all the awareness campaigns I've never heard of inflammatory breast cancer. Did you have risk factors, Kelly? Does breast cancer run in your family?"

"No, I don't have any known risk factors, other than I'm a woman. I was diagnosed out of the blue. One day I was fine, the next morning I found the red area, and within two weeks I was scheduled for a mammogram, biopsy, and diagnosed. I was so scared at the time, I could hardly wait to get some chemo in me."

Jenna's admiration for Kelly was obvious. "Only forty percent of IBC patients make it past five years. But Kelly is a fighter, and I know she's in that forty percent. It seems like after all these years of research, we'd be closer to finding the cause."

Dani looked up from her notes and nodded. "I agree. Did you happen to see my article about the research they're doing at the Rush Institute? It really sounds like they're on to something."

"No, I haven't read anything promising at all. It's about time someone made some progress." Kelly said.

Dani nodded. "So, back to the cost, Kelly. Did the three-hundred thousand dollars you mentioned include reconstructive surgery?"

"No. Because of the type of breast cancer I had, I couldn't have reconstruction at the same time as my mastectomy, as some women do. That was just the cost of getting rid of the cancer." Kelly said.

Dani glanced at a text message on her phone. "Kelly, Jenna I need to get back to the office, but thank you for speaking with me about something so personal. Do you mind if I take your phone numbers in case I need to follow up?"

Fifteen minutes later Dani was sitting at her desk, mulling over what she'd just learned. *Three-hundred thousand dollars?* She did some quick calculations, then jotted down some questions for the candidates.

The University of Denver auditorium was buzzing with security and reporters. After showing her credentials at three checkpoints, she took her seat in the press area and craned her neck to see James pushing through the swarm of photographers to stake his claim to a spot near the stage.

Dani noted some well-known business executives in the audience, chatting, shaking hands, and taking advantage the opportunity to network. Senator Newman's campaign manager was working the crowd; collecting envelopes that she assumed contained campaign contributions.

She recognized a number of people she'd interviewed over the years, and waved at Honey Romano.

When the debate wrapped up, the candidates mingled with the crowd shaking hands, and chatting.

"Senator Newman," Dani waved her hand, and the incumbent senator looked her way. "On the issue of healthcare reform, in my estimate breast cancer treatment in this country costs approximately fifty-billion dollars a year. Does Congress have an interest in funding the ten million dollars needed to get the Rush Institute's breast cancer vaccine to clinical trials?"

"I'm not aware of a vaccine, but any researcher can submit a grant application to the Department of Defense Breast Cancer Research Program." Senator Newman abruptly turned away from her.

She raised her voice, "Senator, this research is being done right here in Denver. Wouldn't this go a long way toward saving lives while reducing healthcare costs for women in every state? Wouldn't it help tremendously with the national debt going forward since the cost of treatment rises every year, and so few can afford it?"

The senator lost himself in the crowd, and a few minutes later she noticed him collecting a number of envelopes from supporters before heading backstage.

"Fifty *billion*?" A local network reporter pushed his way toward her, and several others listened in. "How did you come up with that number?"

"It was a quick estimate, but I believe it to be conservative. An estimated," she checked her notes, "two hundred ninety six thousand women, and over twenty two hundred men will develop breast cancer this year in our country. And the cost of treatment is on the rise."

She looked up to see a growing crowd of reporters around her, and continued. "I spoke with one woman this afternoon whose treatment ran about three-hundred thousand dollars before reconstructive surgery."

Several reporters scribbled on their notepads.

"And there's a vaccine to prevent it?"

"That sounds like a pretty big story," another reporter noted. "How did you come up with this?"

The network reporter wanted more, "Do you have connections at the Rush Institute, or something? I've never heard of this."

She stared at him. "You're kidding. There was a press release sent out about a month ago. In fact, now that I think about it, I wonder why all of you didn't cover this story."

"Must've come in on a big news day." One of the reporters shrugged. "Oh, I do remember reading something about that. You reported on this, didn't you, Dani?"

"I did. The research is encouraging, but unfortunately the lead researcher died as the result of a hit-and-run."

Her phone vibrated with a text from the TV reporter who was standing right in front of her. "Coffee tomorrow?"

She smiled, and texted backed, "What are you up to? Sure, your treat."

He grinned, and stuffed his phone in his pocket. "That's it for me. Good night all."


Dani showered and crept to bed not wanting to wake Charles, but he rolled over and took her in his arms. "I watched the debate, but the TV station went to commercial break just as I heard you asking a question."

"Typical." She rolled over and kissed him deeply. "Ummmmm, I've missed you!"

"Not as much as I missed you." Charles kissed her neck, gently clutched a handful of her hair in one hand, and slipped the other hand to the small of her back.

Taking in a long luxurious breath she sank into him, and covered his full lips with her mouth, aroused by the taste of him, the scent of him.

She rolled on top of him and sat up, grinning down at her husband. "You're looking mighty fine in the moonlight Mr. Driscoll. What's your pleasure?"

"My pleasure? Oh, Mrs. Driscoll you are a tempting little thing." Moving his hands underneath her t-shirt, he rubbed up and down her back then cupped her breasts gently in his hands.

She kissed him again, and nibbled playfully at his lower lip until he pulled her closer.

# CHAPTER 8

Mona arrived at her office with a basket of fruit and cheese, and set it on Jackie's desk. "Good Morning! This is for you dear."

"Mmmm!" Jackie dove in for a chocolate covered strawberry. "Thank you. What's this for?"

"I just wanted you to know how much you're appreciated in this organization. Why don't you get some coffee for both of us, and come to my office?"

Jackie set two cups of coffee on Mona's desk and sat down with her notepad. "New awareness campaign?"

Mona smiled and ran a finger over her broach. "Not today, dear. I had lunch with one of the researchers at the Rush Institute. She was overlooked for a key position after Dr. Jennings' tragic death and is absolutely distraught over it. She needs our help, although I don't know why she'd stay there after such an obvious slight."

"Are you going to approve their grant proposal then?" Jackie asked.

"I can't very well do that now, can I? The primary investigator has died, the current team has very little published research, and no record of any breakthroughs. That changes everything. In fact..."

Mona held up a finger momentarily, and punched an extension. "Kathy, please draft a letter to the Rush Institute that their grant proposal has been denied due to the... How should we put this? Ah, I've got it. The proposal has been denied due to the passing of the primary investigator, Dr. Nolan Jennings. Have it signed by the Chair, and send a copy to Jackie for my files. Thank you Kathy."

Directing her attention back to Jackie, "Dear Bridget suddenly finds herself working under the direction of Seth McCleary. She is heartbroken that the board at Rush overlooked her seniority, but she remains loyal to the research and is in need of a grant writer. Isn't that something your sister-in-law does?"

"Ex sister-in-law. And yes, Keri is a grant writer, but she lives in Fort Collins. That's at least a two-hour commute during rush hour. Would they let her work remotely?"

"I doubt it. She'd need to be in Denver. Please arrange a meeting for me at the earliest possible time."

"I'm sure she'd love to meet with you Mona, but I can't imagine she'd leave Fort Collins and her job at the University."

"One never knows. Set it up please, Jackie. Now, what else is on our schedule?"


Keri Breen nervously rubbed at a scuff on her shoe, huffed a breath on it, and rubbed it again. She was aware of Mona Davenport's high standards and had wanted to meet her for years. The timing had never been quite right, and after she'd divorced Jackie's brother she was sure she'd never get an introduction.

She was giddy knowing that Mona had requested a meeting with her, even though she had no intention of moving to Denver, as Jackie had forewarned her was the topic of the meeting.

She pulled into the parking lot hoping to convince Mona she would be an excellent fit for reviewing grant proposals at the American Pink Ribbon Foundation's Fort Collins office. Reviewing proposals was much faster than writing them, and maybe it could even be done part-time, from home.

She made one last check of her freshly cut bob in the rear view mirror, applied lipstick, and grabbed the folder containing her resume', references, and examples of her work.

The elevator opened to the only suite on the floor.

"Keri dear, so good of you to come on short notice." Mona extended her hand. "It seems we have a lot to discuss. Let's get started, shall we?" She motioned to a chair.

"I'm happy to finally meet you, Ms. Davenport, thank you for having me," Keri said.

"Jackie tells me you are quite a brilliant grant writer. Tell me about that, dear."

Blushing, Keri replied, "Well, I don't know if I'd call myself brilliant, but I do have a high success rate with the proposals I submit. I've learned a lot over the years. I know how to make a proposal stand out, and how to dot the "i's" and cross the "t's". Actually, I'd love to work in your Fort Collins office. I've admired your tenacity and drive to beat this horrible disease for such a long time."

"Thank you, dear. As you probably know, I lost my dear mother to breast cancer. During the time she was sick I discovered one in every eight women in America develops this terrible disease at some point in her life." She fingered her broach. "It seemed appropriate to create a foundation to work for and honor all of those women. I want to make every woman in America feel included in our efforts."

"That's a beautiful sentiment, Ms. Davenport, and you certainly have recruited an impressive number of supporters over the years. I admire that, and I'm anxious to help you in any way I can."

"And you are in a position to do just that, dear. There is a lab right here in Denver working on a cure, but unfortunately they lost their lead researcher to a tragic accident. They are regrouping now to try and keep the research going. I met with Bridget Mallory, one of the researchers–a sweet young woman. I wanted to offer my condolences in person of course, but when I arrived for our appointment I found poor Bridget in such a state."

"I did read about that accident in the Tribune. It's heartbreaking. They were working on a preventive vaccine, weren't they?"

"Yes, well I do think that reporter was a bit out of her depth, but certainly Bridget is dealing with a personal tragedy."

Keri brushed off the odd statement. "Is Bridget okay now? I'm sure they all work closely together. She must be devastated."

"Devastated is right. The Board of Directors looked over poor Bridget, and promoted a lesser colleague to continue the research. Bridget feels betrayed by this Seth McCleary, but she is determined to stick with the research. She's in desperate need of an experienced grant writer."

"I'd love to help, but I'm sure they must want someone to work locally."

"Yes, that's true, dear." Mona back sat in her chair confidently. "You're recently divorced, aren't you? And have no children I assume, since Jackie has never mentioned a niece or nephew. This opportunity is perfect for you in every way."

Slowly shaking her head, "I'm sorry, I'm not following. Why..."

"This is a chance for a brand new start, Keri dear. Come." She motioned to Keri, and walked over to her window overlooking the city. "Denver is a delightful city just brimming with culture and wealthy, well-educated men. Surely an attractive young woman such as yourself would welcome a new start."

Stuttering, "I... Well... I've never thought about relocating. I have a life and a good job at the university in Fort Collins. This is too far for a daily commute, and I don't know if I'd like living in Denver. Besides, there's no guarantee I'd get the job even if I applied."

"Oh, my dear, you must know that a recommendation from me is as good as a golden ticket. I can picture you there already, a vital part of the team at Rush. It's really the perfect solution for you, and for Bridget. Don't you agree?"

Keri adjusted her collar, wondering how to turn this conversation around. "It sounds like a wonderful opportunity for the right person. But honestly, I think I could do a better job working for your foundation. Reviewing proposals in your Fort Collins office."

Mona's nod was almost imperceptible. "That does sound temping, dear, but we have no such position open at the moment." Mona leaned closer, and took Keri's hand. "I'll tell you what we'll do. Let's have you take the position at Rush for... why don't we say a year? After a year, if it's not working to your satisfaction, I'll hold a position open for you here at our Denver office, or relocate you to the Fort Collins office, if you prefer. How does that sound?"

Keri re-played the conversation over and over in her head on the drive home. How could she have agreed to move to another city in the course of a one-hour conversation with a woman she'd just met? It was true she could use a change of scenery to pick up the pieces of her life now that the divorce was final. But, Denver?

Mona smoothed her jacket and picked up the phone. "Bridget Mallory, please. Tell her it's Mona Davenport calling."

# CHAPTER 9

When Seth pulled up to the Jennings residence, the first thing he noticed was that all of the drapes were drawn. He sat in the car for a moment, preparing to see Suzanne for the first time since that awful night.

Suzanne opened the door, her eyes swollen and red. "Come in Seth. Thanks for bringing these things over. I just didn't think I could do it. Putting his things in boxes is like undoing the life Nolan worked so hard to build. Would you put the boxes in Nolan's study please?"

He found her standing in the kitchen when he finished. Her back was turned, shoulders hunched, and shaking. "Why wasn't it me, Seth?" She sobbed. "Why wasn't it me who was struck by that car? Nolan had so much to offer the world."

He wrapped his arms around her and rubbed her back as she wept. "Suz, we never know why these things happen.

We can't predict the future, and we can't change what's past. Nolan wouldn't have wanted you to take his place; he loved you. I know he spent a lot of time at the lab, but one thing I know about Nolan for sure is that he loved you, and he loved his girls. He was proud of his family."

"I know he was. Thank you, Seth." She let go of him and seemed to regain her composure, although he guessed it would be temporary.

"I found some things I thought you should have." She took a large manila envelope off the kitchen counter and handed it to him. "Nolan kept this journal here at the house. He wrote notes, sometimes in the middle of the night." She put her hand over her heart. "His research was never far from his mind. And the flash drives are backups of his office computer files. He never trusted having only one backup. He'd want you to have these."

"Thank you, Suz. I'll do everything in my power to move this vaccine forward and make sure Nolan's name is linked with its success."

"I know you will, Seth. I'm glad the board gave the position to you instead of some stranger. Nolan would be glad to know that, too."

"That means a lot to me. Can I do something for you before I go? Make you some tea? Coffee maybe?"

"No thank you, I'm fine." She looked up at him with sad eyes. "Seth, Nolan considered you a friend, not just a colleague. And, I've come to think of you that way too. I hope you'll stay in touch with me. Drop by and tell me how you're doing from time to time." Her lips quivered, and she squeezed his hand as she walked him to the front door.

"I'm proud to be your friend, Suz. Call me anytime. Whether you need a friend or a shoulder, I'm here for you." He kissed her cheek, and barely keeping himself together, walked to his car.


The first thing Bridget noticed the next morning was Seth moving into Nolan's office. "Good morning Seth. Need any help?" She knew she needed to make peace with the board's decision, and put aside her jealousy. Deep down she knew that Seth was a loyal friend and colleague. She was embarrassed about her initial reaction to his promotion.

He peered over the box he was carrying. "Thanks Bridget. You are the most organized person I know. I'd welcome your help getting set up in here."

She set her glasses on her desk, rolled up the sleeves of her lab coat, and went into the office that no longer belonged to Nolan. Assessing the organization of the large bookcase, she shuffled a few research binders, and began unloading the box that Seth had just set on the floor. "How was Suzanne last night?"

"She seems fragile to me. She cried, and I could tell she'd been crying a lot. She's alone now in that big house. I wonder if she'll stay there?"

"Probably. At least for a while. They raised their girls there, and it must hold many beautiful memories of Nolan and the family."

"Nolan's study looks pristine except for the boxes I carried in. But the emptiness was almost deafening. I don't know if I could live there alone, or not."

Amy barged in with wide eyes. She was listening intently to someone on the portable lab phone. "Oh my gosh, Suzanne are you all right? Wait, yes, he's here." She shoved the phone into Seth's hand.

Bridget rushed to Amy's side, and whispered, "What's happened?"

"Someone broke into her house last night." Amy wrapped her arms around herself. "That's so scary. She's all by herself in that big house now."

"Yes, Seth and I were just discussing that," Bridget said.

A moment later Seth rushed out of the office and tossed his lab coat over his old chair on his way out the door. "I'm going over there, I'll be back as soon as I can."

A Denver police car, an unmarked car, and a crime scene investigation van were parked outside the Jennings' house when Seth drove up. The front door was wide open, so

85

he knocked briefly and stepped into the foyer, heading toward the conversation he heard coming from the kitchen.

A crime scene investigator appeared from around the corner and stepped in front of him, blocking his way. "Stop. You can't come in here. Who are you?"

Seth craned his neck looking for Suzanne. "Pardon me. I'm Seth McCleary. The door was open, and I came to see Mrs. Jennings. She called me a few minutes ago."

"Seth?" Suzanne rushed toward him wearing a bathrobe and slippers. Two Denver Police Detectives followed close behind her. "Seth, thank you for coming."

She turned to the detectives, "Detective Collins, Detective Holt, this is a family friend, Seth McCleary."

Seth offered to shake their hands, but they both declined. He turned to Suzanne and took both of her hands in his. "Are you sure you're okay? Tell me what happened."

"You'll have to take this conversation outside until we've finished searching the house," one of the uniformed policemen told them.

Suzanne nodded and led Seth outside. The detectives followed them.

"As I was telling the detectives, it was around 2 am, I think. I got up to go to the bathroom and heard a noise downstairs. For a few seconds I thought Nolan was home because it sounded like drawers opening in his study, so I called out to him." Her eyes filled with tears, and her voice was unsteady. "Then I realized Nolan is gone and I must be imagining things. So, I tip-toed to the top of the steps and listened to be sure."

She pulled a wad of tissues from the pocket of her robe, and blew her nose.

"Someone broke into Nolan's study?" Seth started for the study, but Detective Holt held out a hand to stop him.

"You've been warned once. You cannot go in the house until we've finished up. This is a crime scene investigation."

"Yes, of course. I wasn't thinking." Seth returned his attention to Suzanne.

"Will it be long, detective?" Suzanne looked exhausted.

"Not much longer. Collins can you check on that?" Detective Holt nodded toward the front door, and continued his questioning. "And you say you didn't recognize the person who bolted out the door?"

"I didn't, no. When I called out to Nolan, whoever it was ran right out the front door. I must've scared him as much as he scared me." Suzanne shook her head, her forehead wrinkled. "The security alarm never went off. Maybe I forgot to set it after you left last night, Seth."

Detective Holt alerted on Suzanne's statement. "You were here last night?"

"Yes, I work... Worked with Dr. Jennings at the Rush Institute. I brought over a couple of boxes of personal belongings from his office."

Collins stood at the front door, motioning them in. "They're packing up now. Let's continue this inside."

"I'll check on those boxes." Holt glanced at his partner and left them standing in the foyer.

Seth could see the sympathy on Detective Collins' face. Her words were authoritative, but he could tell she felt bad for the still-grieving widow. He knew they had to question her while the incident was still fresh in her mind, but Seth feared Suzanne was too fragile to hold up under the pressure of another investigation to give them the information they needed.

Collins continued, "We'll double check the alarms, Mrs. Jennings. Do your security cameras keep recordings, or are they just cameras for you to view outside activity?"

"I forgot about those. Nolan handled the security installation. I can't be sure, but I seem to remember the recordings are kept for something like thirty days. I don't recall seeing a recording machine anywhere in the house though."

Collins said, "Most security companies keep the recordings online now. You should have an access code to a secure website. That's probably the best evidence we're gonna get."

Suzanne wrung the wad of tissues she was holding. "Nolan did all of that. I'm not sure how to access it, or even what the password might be."

"That's no problem. We can contact the security company and get access for an ongoing investigation." Detective Collins went on, "You should familiarize yourself with your security system, Mrs. Jennings. Now tell me again what your husband kept in his study."

"As I said before, he didn't keep anything unusual at all. His laptop, travel diaries, photos, books... Nolan loved to read–was always reading two or three books at a time. He had a couple of framed coin collections, but I did notice they're still on the wall."

"And the boxes Mr. McCleary brought over?"

"I was tired last night, and forgot about them. I haven't opened them yet."

Collins was scribbling notes while she continued her questioning. "No safe? No money? Any other valuables?"

Holt interrupted, "And no boxes, no laptop."

Suzanne hitched in a breath and looked wide-eyed at Seth, then at Detective Holt. "He took Nolan's things? Oh my, I need to sit down."

Seth led her to the kitchen table. She was clearly struggling to hold herself together as she quickly brushed away a single tear that trickled down her cheek.

Holt continued, "Apparently, whoever it was saw an opportunity. I'll need a description of the laptop." He turned to Seth, "Were those boxes labeled or identifiable in any way?"

Seth shrugged. "They were just file boxes I picked up from Staples. Bridget labeled them with "Rush Institute", but there was nothing of monetary value. Framed diplomas, some personal photos, a couple of coffee cups. You know, the usual stuff that ends up in someone's office."

"We'll need a list of what was in those boxes, as detailed as possible. And we'll need your prints since you were here last night. Can you come by the station today?" Holt handed him a business card.

"Of course. I have prints on file from the background investigation Rush ran when I was hired." Seth looked at his watch. "I should call the office and let them know I'll be awhile."

Holt directed another question at Suzanne. "Is that the laptop?" He motioned toward an open laptop sitting on the coffee table in the family room.

"No, we each have one. That one's mine." Suzanne seemed to be regaining her composure. "Nolan kept his computer in his study. He rarely worked on it anywhere else."

Holt continued, "It appears the boxes and the laptop are the only things missing. I'm guessing he would have gone for the coin collections next, but you spooked him. The crime scene team got a partial footprint, and we have prints, though they might not belong to the perpetrator." Holt swallowed the rest of the cold coffee he'd left on the kitchen counter. "And you feel certain that you only saw one person run out the door?"

"Yes, I only saw one man. I think it was a man, he was wearing a hoodie." Suzanne shivered and pulled her robe tighter.

"Okay, we have what we need for now. Collins, go see if crime scene's wrapped up."

Detective Holt turned to Suzanne. "Here's my card, Mrs. Jennings. Sometimes people think of things when they're calmer. After events have had some time to sink in. Meantime, we'll talk to the neighbors, and check out the security recordings. If you notice anything else missing or think of anything at all, it would help us find who did this."

Suzanne collapsed on the sofa when the police had all gone. She was still in her robe and slippers, and looked even frailer than last night. "Seth, could you sit with me a moment? I want to run something by you."

"Of course, Suz. Why don't I make some coffee?"

He brought her toast, a sliced apple, and a fresh cup of coffee, and set it on the coffee table in front of her. "Suz, you look exhausted. Are you afraid to be here alone? Maybe one of your daughters should come and stay for a few days."

"No, Seth I'm fine, really. I called you because I was wondering something to myself as the detectives were asking questions, but I didn't want to sound crazy, or paranoid, on top of everything else."

"Does this have to do with the break in?"

She took an apple slice and held it in her hand. "Seth, do you think it's possible that whoever came in here last night was looking for the information in Nolan's journal, or on those backups I gave you?"

His blew out a long whistle. "I guess it's possible. Whoever it was did take the boxes marked with "Rush." And they took Nolan's laptop. You said you heard them opening drawers, so maybe they were looking for something specific."

Seth continued, "I locked the envelope in the filing cabinet when I went in this morning. I haven't even looked to see what's in it yet. Did Nolan keep any other records of his research here?"

"I don't think so. Nothing except the journal, but you're welcome to look. He brought a backup home every evening, but he always put it on the hall table with his keys. I never saw him plug it into the computer here. He kept two flash drives—the ones I gave you. He always left one here, and took the other back to the lab in the morning. He alternated them, saying it was an extra precaution in case something went wrong with the backups at the lab."

"That was a good idea. But I'm wondering... Who do you think would have gone to this extreme?"

Suzanne shook her head thoughtfully. "No one that I am aware of. It's probably just my imagination. I don't know, maybe I'm making more of this than I should. It' s just a feeling, nothing more, but take care of that journal, will you Seth?"

# CHAPTER 10

"This stuff is useless! Junk! Give me the laptop." His employer was furious, and that didn't usually bode well for Alistair Snipes.

"I did the job." Snipes muttered, and handed over the laptop. He paced around the abandoned bowling alley. "Hey, I found some bowling balls, wanna wager who can knock down the most pins?"

He was met with silence, and continued digging around, kicking trash and debris, and pocketing some coins he found on the floor. *Guess you're too hoity-toity for bowling.*

His palms were starting to sweat. The deal was to deliver the computer, and anything else that looked important in a scientific sorta way. The boxes were marked "Rush Institute" so he'd grabbed them. He couldn't help it the bitch woke up and he had to leave in a hurry. He'd held up his end of the deal, and he deserved to be paid.

He wandered around, and found the bathrooms. Filthy, but they would do. On the north end of the main bowling alley he found a couple of offices and a big empty room with a doorway leading to a utility room with electrical panels, furnace, and hot water heater. He toggled one of the circuit breakers, and a few lights flickered on.

"What are you doing?" The angry voice shouted loudly from the main area. "Come here."

"There's nothing on here of any use to me. Destroy it. Get rid of all of it, along with that car before someone recognizes it."

Snipes snatched the laptop and envelope, licked his thumb, ran it through the stack of bills, and slowly nodded. *Looks like it's all here.*

He turned his attention to his employer. "Anything else?"

"No, not for you. What I need is in that lab."

"The Rush lab? I can do that, but it'll cost ya a lot more than this." Snipes held up the envelope.

"The security there is too sophisticated. Keep that cell phone handy, understood? And clean yourself up. Don't you have any self respect?"

Snipes knew an insult when he heard one, but the money was good. He nodded, stuffed the laptop into one of the boxes, and carried it all out the back door. *I could get through that security, how hard could it be?*

He pulled the battered Coup Deville beside the dumpster outside the old bowling alley, looked around for cars, saw none, and opened the trunk. Rummaging through the first box filled with framed diplomas, certificates, and magazine articles, he shook his head and tossed it into the dumpster. *Junk is right. This guy was full of himself. Who frames magazine articles of themselves?* He shook his head. *Disgusting!*

Snipes set the laptop in the trunk, pocketed the cash, and sifted through the second box. Nodding, he pulled out a coffee cup, an expensive-looking pen and pencil set, then hefted the remaining contents into the dumpster. He picked up the laptop, and rubbed his hands over it. *Souvenir. I can use a computer. No way I'm tossin' this in the dumpster.*

Balancing a fast-food lunch, coffee cup, and power cord on top of the laptop, Snipes let himself in the house. The screen door slammed behind him.

Settling down on the worn sofa he bit off a quarter of the hamburger, and opened the laptop. *Let's see what we got.* He dragged a file full of vacation photos to the computer's trash bin, and scanned the hard drive for anything interesting. *Home Security. What's this?*

Opening the file with a click he found a website link, and a document with a passcode. His eyes grew wide when he accessed a series of dated video files. Snipes clicked on the video dated with the current date, stuffed his mouth full of fries, and watched absolutely nothing happening outside the back door. *Boring.* The next video was a view of the front door. He fast-forwarded to one-thirty am, and finished his sandwich. After a few minutes he saw himself pick the lock on the front door, open it slowly, and enter the house.

He tipped up half a can of beer, burped, and watched himself running from the house, balancing the two boxes and laptop.

A message popped up on the computer screen. "Are you sure you want to delete this file? This action cannot be undone."

"Oh, I'm sure, all right." *Delete.*

*Yeah! Good luck finding any evidence now. Lady Luck is on my side. I should make a little trip to Vegas. Let's see what else is on here.*

# CHAPTER 11

"Seth?" Bridget propped herself against the doorway of Seth's office clutching a piece of paper. "I have good news and bad news. Which do you want to hear first?"

Looking up from the computer, Seth massaged his eyes with his palms then looked up at her. "Bad news? I can't take bad news at the moment. What's the good news?"

"Mona Davenport knows a grant writer in Fort Collins who is considering a move to Denver. I've got her resume. She's been writing grants at C.S.U., and she's well qualified. Shall I set up an interview?"

"That is good news." He teetered back precariously in his chair, and ran his hands through his hair, reminding her of Nolan. "I'm swamped with getting Nolan's research moving forward, but it would be great if we could get a grant writer in here quickly."

He stared back at the computer screen. "I thought this would be a breeze. Nolan and I talked so often I thought I knew where he was going with this next, but I'm finding it more challenging than I expected."

Bridget sat down in front of Seth's desk and stuffed her glasses into her pocket. "It would be hard for anyone, Seth. Nolan was unconventional in his approach; he was such a freethinker. It's no wonder another researcher didn't conceptualize prevention the way he did."

She continued, "Everyone else is working on curative drugs, and dosing radiation. But this... Nolan's vaccine, our vaccine is a blessing to women. Our little ones haven't exhibited any side effects at all, and not a one has developed breast cancer. Can you imagine the impact this will have? You can move this forward, Seth. I know you can."

He glanced back at his computer screen shaking his head. "Nolan was a genius, pure and simple. I ran the experiments and made the adjustments with him. I know this like the back of my hand, but I'm missing the next step."

"Can I help?" Bridget had too much respect for the research, and for Seth, to turn her back on it.

He hesitated for a moment. "Bridget, would it be too much to ask of you to handle the interviewing, and hiring? It's important to get someone in here as soon a possible, before our funding runs out. You know what we need as well as I do."

"Sure, I'm happy to handle it. And honestly Seth, I'm

glad it's not me sitting behind this desk." She pushed herself up. "But I'm very happy that you are."

"Thank you, Bridget. For your confidence, and for pitching in to get someone hired. As soon as you have the right person I'll sign off on the paperwork."

"I'm on it." She started out the door.

"Wait! You said you had bad news." He gestured with his fingers, "Let me have it."

Bridget turned and slid the paper across the desk. "I almost forgot. The Pink Ribbon Foundation turned down our application for funding."

"Did she say why?" He grabbed the rejection letter, and scanned over it.

"The letter's not from Mona, it's from the Chairman of her advisory board. Basically, it implies a lack of confidence without Nolan." She saw panic on his face. "Don't worry, we'll get a grant writer in here, and we'll get this funded. You focus on fine-tuning for the next phase. I'll let you get back to work."

Relocating to Denver was easier than Keri imagined, thanks to the personal assistant Mona had hired for her. She'd hardly had to lift a finger except to make decisions: what to pack, sell, or give away, and which of the three pre-screened rentals to move into. Everything else was handled; movers, a crew to unpack, utilities were turned on, and the kitchen was stocked with groceries. Power and money sure could provide a lot of convenience, not to mention those special golden tickets.

Security at The Rush Institute was impressive after the laid back atmosphere of the university. The official offer of employment had been subject to a background check by the Colorado Bureau of Investigation, and the FBI. Keri's first three hours were spent in orientation, signing non-disclosure and non-compete agreements, after which she was ushered to a studio for a security badge photo.

She took the elevator to the third floor lab and swiped her badge in the security reader for the first time. Amy turned around and welcomed her with a smile.

"Welcome, Keri. Bridget is down the hall but she'll be right back. Let me show you where you'll be working."

Seth emerged from his office and shook her hand. "Welcome to the Jennings lab, Keri. We're happy to have you. Bridget is quite impressed with your experience."

"Thank you, Dr. McCleary. I appreciate your confidence. From what I know so far, you should be high on the list for funding from a number of sources."

"We hope so. And please call me Seth."

Amy pointed to the small desk and chair. "For now, you'll be in Seth's old space."

"Thank you. A computer and printer are really all I need. Are you still calling it the Jennings lab? I thought..."

Bridget arrived in time to hear her question. "It's been an emotional transition for us, and Seth wants to keep Nolan's name associated with the research." She nodded toward him. "One day he may change his mind but until then—well he's the boss."

Seth seemed a little embarrassed. "And today the boss wants to take all of you out to lunch. Amy, why don't you help Keri get settled? We'll leave in an hour."

Lunch was delicious, and her new colleagues chatted easily, teasing and poking each other. Keri tried, but couldn't detect a bit of animosity between Bridget and Seth. However, she did notice the sparkle in Amy's eyes when she looked at her boss. *Noted.*

They discussed the next phase of research, as well as the funding sources they were focused on. Keri shared some of her own ideas, obviously impressing Bridget.

"Nolan loved his bench work but loathed writing grants. Maybe with your expertise, Keri, we'll be able to move this to clinical trials soon," Bridget said.

Seth chewed the last of his fries. "I'm still working on some fine tuning, though the findings so far have been outstanding. If only I could somehow tap into Nolan's thought process. I can tell I'm missing something important, and I..." Seth's eyes shifted toward the ceiling, then riveted on Bridget.

"Damn! How could I be so stupid?"

"Seth?" Amy stared at him.

He began speaking so fast that Keri had to lean in to follow. "The journal! Bridget, remember I told you Suzanne gave me the journal Nolan kept at home? She said he stayed up late some nights making notes. And actually, Suzanne was afraid… Never mind. I forgot all about Nolan's journal, until now."

Bridget put her fork down and pushed her plate back. "Do you think Nolan actually kept formulas in that journal?"

"I don't know, but we can hope."

Bridget looked around the table. "Is everyone finished?"

Amy was up in a flash, tugging Seth up from his chair, her ponytail swinging. "Yes, let's go!"

# CHAPTER 12

Dani sat at the breakfast table with Charles, staring at the text message on her phone. "No coffee today, sry."

She shook her head and sent her own text. "I'll buy, np."

"Producer says no story."

"It's a big story. Meet anyway?"

"Short on time, sry."

Dani slumped in her chair with an exasperated sigh. "I don't understand."

Charles peered over the morning paper. "What don't you understand, sweetheart?"

"First Coop edited my debate story, which he hardly ever does. Now the TV reporter cancelled our meeting because apparently his producer thinks there's no story. I even tried to comment on a discussion about breast cancer on

Facebook, and my comment was deleted—I assume by the group monitor. What's going on?"

"I thought your article on the debate was informative, but I didn't realize it was edited. What are you getting at?"

"The Jennings vaccine. No one wants to talk about it, much less cover it. Isn't it big news?"

Charles folded the newspaper and put it on the table. "Seems like big news to me, but what do I know about medical research. Maybe it's flawed."

"It's not flawed!" Her tone was sharper than she intended it to be, and she grabbed her pencil and tapped it furiously on the table. "Charles, why would you say it's flawed? It's already been proven 100% effective in preventing breast cancer in mice. Bridget said even the mice that were bred to develop the disease didn't develop it after receiving the vaccine. This is a huge breakthrough."

He reached across the table and stopped her tapping pencil. "If it's such a big success then the Rush Institute will get behind it, they're huge."

"It takes funding, Charles. Bridget explained that Rush uses the funds they raise for overhead. To pay for employees, building expenses, administration—that kind of thing. The researchers are responsible for securing grants to fund their own projects."

"Then surely Mona will fund it. Or one of the thousands of other organizations raising money for breast cancer these days."

"Well, we already know that Mona is annoyed about it, for some reason. Something isn't right, Charles. I have an uneasy feeling in the pit of my stomach. I've tried to make sense of her response, but no matter how I try, I can't do it. Coop won't print it. Now our sister station says there's no story. It doesn't make any sense."

"Have you discussed this with Pete? Medical's his turf, maybe he has some insight."

"No. I don't want him to think I'm moving in on his territory. Not that I'm any threat on the medical beat." She grinned, relaxing a bit. "There was a reason why I didn't major in science."

"You're smarter than you give yourself credit for, Sweetheart." Charles said.

He topped off their coffee, and changed the subject. "What other stories are you working on?"

"I was actually invited to cover the ribbon cutting for that software company you financed. Will you be there?"

"Yes I will. And I'll take you to lunch afterwards."

Lowering her head, and batting her eyelashes, "Why, Mr. Driscoll, are you asking me out on a date?"

He rolled up the paper and tapped her on the head with it. "Yes, Mrs. Driscoll, I surely am. And I must confess, my intentions are less than honorable."

"That's my guy!" She giggled.

# CHAPTER 13

"What's your opinion, Honey? Is there any reason to think the research is flawed?" Dani had run into Honey at the coffee shop by chance. The timing was perfect.

Honey dipped biscotti into a steaming cup of coffee, and bit off a piece. "Not that I'm aware of. Shouldn't you speak with Mona Davenport about this, though? You know I'm not a fan of hers, but she has a scientific advisory board, and they would be in a better position to analyze this that I am."

Knowing she needed to be careful what she revealed, Dani continued. "I spoke with Bridget at the lab last week. She told me The American Pink Ribbon Foundation has turned down their funding request, stating the death of the lead researcher as the official reason."

"Well, that does sound like a legitimate reason to me. Did I tell you I sent a contribution to the Rush lab after we spoke last?

"No, you didn't mention it. That's wonderful, Honey."

Honey nodded. "I'm so encouraged by the news that someone is finally focusing on prevention. If this vaccine is as successful in women as it is in mice, it could save my little girls from the awful treatments I went through. That's worth everything to me."

Dani looked up from her notes and smiled. "My best guess is that your donation is being put to good use. They promoted one of the researchers in the lab to carry on as principal investigator. I met all of them when I was there, and they seemed to know the research inside and out."

"That's excellent news." Honey rifled through her handbag and pulled out a notepad. "Who's the lead researcher now?"

"Dr. Seth McCleary. I understand he is also a friend of the Jennings family, though I haven't spoken with him directly since he took the position. I need to call them again."

Honey poised her pen over the notepad. "When will your story print?"

Shifting in her chair and hesitating, Dani admitted, "I don't actually have this story approved yet."

"You don't?" Honey finished her coffee and pushed back her chair. "Well, it's a big breakthrough, I'm sure you'll get it approved."

Dani got out of her car that evening, waved at the SUV driving by, then flopped down on the porch swing with a heavy sigh.

"Coming in this evening, or are you planning a campout on the front porch?" Charles stood at the front door teasing her.

"It's been a long day between work and my own research on the Rush story. I ran into Honey at D'Angelo's this morning, and chatted with her over coffee. That put me a little behind at the paper, so I didn't take time for lunch. I'm starving, and at all not motivated to cook. I have too much on my mind."

"Want to walk to Rossetti's for pizza?"

"Mmmmm!" Pushing up off the swing, and wrapping her arms around her husband's neck, she answered, "You're my hero, once again!"


The waiter had barely set the pizza in front of them before Dani slid a large slice onto her plate, and then turned toward the door when the bell announced another customer. She smiled and waived at the muscular Denver Police Detective before he could be seated. "Terrell! Pull up a chair, we have plenty."

Detective Terrell Holt had been the first person to welcome them to Washington Park when they bought their house three years ago. They were unpacking, and he had stopped by on the last day he wore a police uniform, and presented them with a Neighborhood Watch flyer, and a pepperoni pizza from Rossetti's.

Terrell was one of those people you instantly liked, unless you were a criminal. As it turned out he lived across the street. It was obvious to Dani that his long awaited promotion to detective was also well deserved.

The two men shook hands, and Charles motioned for the waiter to bring another beer. "Off duty?"

"Yup, just got off. I haven't talked to you two in weeks. How's it going?"

"Business loans are picking up. I just looked at a proposal for a new development north of the city. The old bowling alley property off I-25–you know the place." Charles said.

"Yeah, I know that dump." Terrell dug in to a slice of pizza. "It'll be good to see that place cleaned up, and developed. We get some undesirables hanging out in that old place, now and then. How about you Dani-girl? Big news day?"

"Enough to keep me more than busy," Dani said. "I hope your day was quiet. A quiet day for you is a good day for our neighborhood."

"Low crime, and a great Neighborhood Watch program are my favorite things about living in Wash Park. Hey, what're you guys doin' tonight? I just picked up a movie. Care to join me?"

Dani pushed back from the table. "I'd love to get my mind off work for awhile. Let's take the rest of the pizza."

Charles pulled out his wallet to pay the check. "Whatever makes my wife happy."


Terrell made popcorn, gathered three bottles of beer from the refrigerator, and set one in front of Dani. "What are you working on that's got you all riled up, girlie? Some new business polluting the planet?"

She giggled. He knew her well. "No. I'm digging into a story that's got me baffled."

"Yeah, and she's doing it on her own time. She's obsessed," Charles teased.

Dani told them about her meeting with Honey, and what she'd dug up so far. "I hate to say this because it sounds awful, but I'm beginning to think breast cancer is such a big business that no one really wants a prevention."

"Awww, Dani-girl. That sounds terrible. Still, what I've learned in my years on the force is there's corruption in every industry. But breast cancer?" He shook his head, and reached for a handful of popcorn. "That's just a shame. They say money's at the root of all evil, though. And we know there's a lot of money changing hands in that industry. Money is power these days."

He knit his eyebrows together. "Hey, why'd you say you're doing the legwork for this on your own time? Seems like hard times at the Trib if can't pay its reporters."

"All I can say is, it a sensitive topic at the Trib." Dani slid of her shoes and folded her legs on the sofa.

Charles patted her thigh. "It's keeping her up at night, that's for sure. I've asked her to let it go, but this has a hold on her for some reason."

She nearly choked on her pizza. "Some reason? Charles this affects over a quarter of a million women every single year! What if I came home one day and told you I had breast cancer?"

"Sweetheart! Don't say that." Charles looked horrified. "I'm sorry. I know this is important, but realistically I don't see how you can make an impact if Coop won't print the story."

"What did I miss? The Trib won't print a story about breast cancer? That seems unusual. Did you piss off the editor, or what?" Terrell asked.

"No, I..." She slumped down into the sofa with her beer. "Let's just watch the movie."

# CHAPTER 14

Seth bolted through the door to his office. He fumbled for the keys to the filing cabinet, nearly dropped them, and finally jerked open the top drawer and dumped the contents of the envelope onto his desk.

Bridget, Amy, and Keri stood eyeing the considerable size of the journal while he flipped through the first few pages.

"I recognize these notes and graphs from a few years ago." He turned the pages carefully.

"That will take some time to get through." Bridget said. "Why don't Amy and I get Keri up to speed while you're going through that?"

"I just know the information you need is in there." Amy flashed a smile at Seth. "Let us know if you find something."

He nodded and sank down in his chair, feeling uneasy about reading Nolan's inner most thoughts on the research.

Guilt and elation fought for control of his emotions. Seeing Nolan's precise handwriting on the pages before him made his breath hitch. *Nolan would have wanted this. He'd have wanted his research to continue.*

It was obvious to Seth that some passages were corrected after findings in the lab revealed a better outcome than Nolan expected, but the journal detailed the research thoroughly. Flipping to the back of the journal, he read the last few pages. He sat up straighter, furrowed his brow, and turned back a few pages more.

"This is it! I've got it!" Scrambling out of his chair, he was in the lab holding out the journal for Bridget to see before she could move from her spot.

"And look, there's even more. Nolan wanted to be sure the dosage for every element was safe for women before he took it to trial. See? References to safety on every substance we use are here."

Bridget took the journal from his shaking hand, and grinned at him. "We can't see while you're waving it all over the place."

She sat down at her desk with the journal, shoving her glasses on while he and the others peered over her shoulder. "Oh Seth, this research is more important than Nolan told any of us." She ran her fingers over lines of carefully penned notes. "I knew he was determined to ensure the success of the phase one trials, but look." She pointed to a list of cancers written in Nolan's hand. "Nolan thought this could be adapted to other cancers."

Amy's eyes widened. "He was that far ahead of what we were doing here in the lab?"

"So far ahead." Seth paced back and forth, anxious to get his hands on the journal again.

"Nolan had no idea that he was leaving us a gift when he recorded these notes." Bridget turned the pages with the same reverence Seth had used.

Amy wrapped her arms around his neck. "Seth, you're in business!"

"We're all in business."

He glanced at Keri, who was silently peering over Bridget's shoulder, obviously trying to process what was happening.

"Keri, to be honest I was struggling with how to move this forward with the expected improvements while we're waiting on funding. Nolan wanted it fined tuned, even though our success thus far has been 100%. It turns out that he had already taken the research many steps forward, at least on paper. He was moving faster than we could prove his theories."

Amy nodded. "And knowing Nolan, he probably didn't tell us so we wouldn't be tempted to skip steps, or get ahead of ourselves. He always wanted his research carefully executed and documented."

Keri nodded. "That's wonderful. I just need to read over the research so I can begin submitting proposals. Bridget gave me a flash drive with the older proposals, but I'd like to review the notes for myself."

"Good idea, fresh set of eyes." Amy smiled at their new colleague. She pointed to the journal Bridget was still thumbing through. "Do you want me to record those notes in the database for you?"

Reaching for the journal, and hefting it up and down in his hands, he replied. "No, I can get into Nolan's head better if I do it myself. It's gonna be a long night."

Keri's cell phone rang just as she pulled into the driveway.

"Keri dear, it's Mona. I wanted to call and see if you enjoyed your first day at the Rush Institute."

"Hello Mona. I just got home. It was a busy day, actually. Bridget and Amy are great, and I think Seth caught his stride on the research today." She let herself in the front door, and slung her handbag on the sofa.

"I'm glad you enjoyed your day, dear. I'm sure you'll find Denver a bit more exciting than Fort Collins. This could prove to be an enormous opportunity for you."

"I have to admit, you're probably right. Thank you for using one of your golden tickets on my behalf." She tucked the phone under her chin, and poured a glass of iced tea from the refrigerator.

"I was happy to help. Now tell me dear, what did you mean when you said Mr. McCleary caught his stride today?"

"It's Dr. McCleary actually. He found Dr. Jennings' journal on the research after lunch. Apparently, Dr. Jennings' wife gave Seth the journal, but he locked it up in the filing cabinet, and forgot about it."

"Interesting. And he found the information helpful, I presume?"

"Very helpful. They have high expectations for this research, and as soon as I get up to speed I'll be sending you another proposal with Seth listed as primary investigator. I need to read over the research myself first, but it does sound exciting. We only need ten million dollars to produce the vaccine and fund phase one clinical trials. I can't think of anyone better suited to fund it."

"That's a lovely thought, dear. I look forward to receiving your proposal. We're revising the submittal guidelines, and I'll be sure to have Jackie send you a copy when they're finalized. Send her your new email address, will you, dear?"

"I will. It was so nice of you to call Mona."

"You're most welcome."

"And Keri," Mona continued. "I know it will take some time for you to get up to speed with your new position. Why don't you send me the full research documentation so my review board will have a jump-start when we receive your application? Confidentially, of course."

"Oh, that would be great, Mona. I'll ask Seth if..."

"Nonsense, dear! Dr. McCleary is far too busy for trivial details. That's why he hired you. Take the initiative, Keri. Send me the documents, and I can promise you an expeditious response to your proposal when I receive it. We'll keep this confidential, between the two of us, and you'll soon have earned that reputation as a brilliant grant writer. Now do take care dear, and enjoy your evening."

Click.

Keri stared at the phone in her hand for a moment, and shrugged.

# CHAPTER 15

Mona Davenport smoothed her skirt, tugged at her jacket, and walked purposefully into the large conference room. She stood at the head of the table, acknowledged each of her board members in turn, and she sat down with a radiant smile.

"Welcome to a special session of the American Pink Ribbon Advisory Board. I hope you enjoyed a productive discussion with Mr. Hastings this morning, and have had the opportunity to consider the concept I developed, and couriered to your homes last week."

Heads nodded around the extravagant table.

"Is there any further discussion?" She asked.

Gary Walker, an Oncologist from Illinois expressed his concern. "This is a rather abrupt diversion from our usual modus operandi. Is anyone else concerned that it will affect the status of the foundation?"

Mona held up her hand, "No, no. I have our attorney's working on the legalities as we speak. Let's leave the legal matters to the them, and the funding to me, shall we?" She flashed a confident smile and looked to her most avid supporter. "Mr. Hastings, do you care to comment?"

Todd Hastings, Co-Chair of the advisory board, stood up to address them. "Mona and I have been working on this around the clock, and we believe it's the best way forward. This concept is the best way to control the situation, and accomplish the stated goals of the foundation." He paused, looking around the table. "Now listen carefully. Each of us sitting here has quite a lot at stake unless we take a leadership position in this now. You all must understand that enormous profits are at risk here. Hell, the stability of our companies may be on the line. We'll be bleeding revenue, and shareholders will be down our throats if we don't take advantage of this opportunity. You all know it's true. The time is now—or it may be never."

"Thank you Todd." Mona sipped her water, and looked around the table at some of the most brilliant minds in science; scholars, researchers, drug manufacturers, and oncologists on a mission to make a name for themselves. She had sought them out personally when building her advisory board, understanding the perks that come with affiliation.

"My dear board members, you all know time is of the

essence. Mr. Hastings and I feel strongly that we must move forward with developing and funding our own research, as outlined in the documents before you."

Mona placed her hands on the table and leaned forward, lowering her voice to assure she had their undivided attention. "Postponing this decision will impact all of us in our own personal and professional endeavors. This advisory board possesses the talent and resources necessary to carry this through on our own timetable. Otherwise, I'm afraid we may all be out of business."

Peering around the room, she sat back and folded her hands. "All in favor?"

# CHAPTER 16

The aroma of coffee and bacon wafted up the stairs, and Dani stretched lazily and smiled. *Saturday at last.*

"Wake up sleepy head." Charles sat on the side of the bed holding two cups of coffee.

"What time is it?" She reached for a cup and smelled the rich aroma.

"Almost nine. It's about time you got a good night's sleep. You didn't budge an inch when I got up and showered."

"It took me awhile to fall asleep, so I got up and organized some of my thoughts from last night. Once I had it all down on paper, I crashed. I feel surprisingly refreshed." she grinned up from her cup, and raised her eyebrows. "Do I smell bacon?"

"Hickory smoked bacon, blueberry pancakes, and maple syrup from the farmer's market. Hungry?"

"Mmmmm. Yes. It smells delicious." She handed him her cup. "Let me brush my teeth, and I'll be right down."

Swirling a piece of bacon in maple syrup contemplatively, she decided to run her idea past Charles. "You know, I still want to get this story out, and I have an idea. What about a blog? A personal blog won't violate my contract with the Trib if I'm careful."

"I'm not so sure about that. Coop told you the subject is closed, and I doubt he'd appreciate a rant on the Internet from one of his reporters."

She bit her lip. "True. Then what about a pseudonym? No one would know who was writing, and I can't think of any reason why Coop would ever find it online. He wants nothing to do with the subject at the moment."

Charles nodded. "I think that might work, but Sweetheart are you sure you won't just let this go? Let the marketing department at Rush handle the publicity and fund raising. That's their job."

"I hear you, Charles, I really do. But, I want women to know it might be possible to actually prevent breast cancer. I want to rescue the city from all those," she waved her hand in the air with disgust, "pink ribbons that are blanketing the city again. It's hard for me to believe that none of the charities have gotten behind the Jennings research. No one seems to have heard about it, and I think it's because the media is refusing to cover it. Why is that, Charles?"

"I don't know. It does seem to be a mystery, unless this vaccine's not all it's cracked up to be. That would explain everything, wouldn't it? Isn't it possible that no one will fund this project because the research isn't up to standard?"

"It's The Rush Institute. Of course it's credible. They would never risk their reputation by going public with their results unless they were confident."

Charles looked skeptical, and shrugged.

Dani continued, "Okay, I'll concede to the possibility that maybe the research team got ahead of itself, and announced a little too early. But, how can you argue with one hundred percent success? Whatever the reason, this is not being embraced as a breakthrough, and I intend to find out why. And in all fairness I'll blog about it either way. The blog will give me an outlet for my frustrations."

"Fair enough," he picked up their plates and bent over to kiss the top of her head. "I'll clean up while you set up your blog."

*Best blog formats*, she typed into the search engine, and decided on a Wordpress blog. *Oh, this is fun.* She selected a design, breezed through the customization sections, and sat there looking at the blank screen. Where to start?

About You. "Rogue reporter on a mission," she typed. *No, I need anonymity. Something catchy, something women will find online. Pink Ribbons? No, too common, it'll get buried.*

*Hope, Incorporated.* She pursed her lips, nodded, and started typing.

# CHAPTER 17

Dani walked to D'Angelo's for lunch, and settled into a booth with coffee and a sandwich. Though she couldn't very well interview Seth McCleary from her office at the Tribune, there was nothing wrong with making some calls on her own time.

"Hello, Jennings lab. Keri Breen speaking."

Knitting her eyebrows together, Dani thought, *why do I recognize that name?* "Hello Keri, this is Dani Driscoll, is Dr. McCleary available?"

"He's at lunch. Is there something I can help you with?"

"No, I don't think so. Is Bridget in, by chance?"

"I'm afraid it's just me. May I leave them a message?"

"No, I'll call back, thank you." She bit her lip, and tucked her phone back inside her handbag. *Keri Breen, Keri*

*Breen… I know that name from somewhere.*

"There you are. I haven't seen you since breakfast." Looking up, she noticed Charles had his walking shoes on. "I guess I don't need to ask what you're working on."

"I've uncovered something disconcerting." She tapped her pencil on the table, and continued. "I called the lab at Rush yesterday to find out how the transition was going with Dr. McCleary, and the person who answered the phone was new. As soon as she said her name I was sure I'd heard it before. And I had."

Charles got comfortable in the upholstered chaise that Dani often curled up on to read. "Are you going to make me guess?"

She giggled. "No, I'll tell you. Keri Breen has connections to Mona's foundation. She's the sister-in-law of Mona's executive assistant. I looked her up. Recently divorced, supporter of the foundation, and played tennis in every one of the foundation's Fort Collins tournaments for the last decade."

"And that's a problem because?" Charles asked.

"I can't be sure yet, but don't you think it's an unlikely coincidence?" Dani could tell Charles was still concerned about her digging into this, but at this point she felt compelled to sort this out, if only for her own peace of mind.

She continued, "There's more. A lot more. I've found

some unsettling information, or at least it's disturbing to me. I've been digging into various charities raising money on behalf of breast cancer, and there are tens of thousands of them. Some are supporting research, some support services for patients, but a surprising number of them are not registered non-profits at all."

"Maybe some of the smaller charities are individuals who care, and want to help." Charles said.

"Maybe. But the problem is there's no accountability. I've dug into dozens of them already. A lot of these so call charities are nothing more than businesses. They personally profit by designing and selling awareness merchandise with not a penny going toward breast cancer."

She turned around and looked at her husband. "I stopped at the store on my way home last night, and bought some light bulbs for the front porch. The package has a pink ribbon on it. I noticed pink ribbons on all sorts of products. These ribbons seem to have morphed into a scheme to increase sales of merchandise. It's disgusting."

"And look." Dani turned back to her computer, and clicked on one of about thirty URL's she had dragged to her desktop. "The top ten breast cancer charities in the U.S. raised over a billion and a half dollars last year. Well over half of the money raised was divided between awareness, salaries, and overhead. And look," she clicked on a spreadsheet, "some of these executives collect exorbitant salaries, which makes me wonder about their motives."

Charles leaned in, raising his brow. "I have to agree those are enormous salaries for organizations set up as charities."

"And charities are only a small part of the problem." She pointed to the columns on her spreadsheet. "All of these businesses make astronomical profits from these women. Breast cancer is a business, Charles. A big, profitable business."

"It is, of course. But these companies also serve the sick, and provide cures. They're professionals, and business people. I understand there are unscrupulous people in nearly every large business, but that doesn't necessarily make the entire industry bad. You know, one bad apple, and such."

"Well, I think there's more than one bad apple in this case," she said.

He stood up and kissed her cheek. "Looks like you're up to your elbows in this."

"I am. I'm trying to find out why, after billions and billions of dollars have been raised over decades, prevention hasn't already been discovered, and developed. The statistics for these women haven't improved a bit. Do you want to know what my conclusion is?"

"I'll bite. What's your conclusion?" Charles asked.

"I've concluded there is simply no financial incentive for any of these businesses or charities to fund prevention.

There's more profit for them in continuing down the path of funding cures. But the cures are toxic drugs that create an even bigger industry. The side effects last a lifetime, which sucks. Some of these treatments sound more like torture to me. One blog I found described the treatments as poison, burn, and mutilate."

"That's a bold conclusion, but I can see how you've reached it. Maybe someone will step forward with funding for the Rush research." He offered her a hand. "In the meantime, it's nice outside, and today's the last Farmers Market of the season. Let's walk to the park, and see what's left."

She stood up, stretched, and wrapped her arms around his waist. "I guess I need a break."


Walking briskly through crisp autumn air, colorful leaves fluttering at their feet, Dani felt invigorated. "I love the sound of the leaves crunching under my feet." She zipped her windbreaker and pulled up her collar. "The air smells of Fall, and fireplaces. It's getting chilly. I wonder if we'll have rain for Halloween this year."

"Seems to happen more often than not in Denver." Checking the calendar on his iPhone, he nodded. "Halloween is in two weeks, want to carve some pumpkins tonight?"

Dani took his hand with a bounce in her step. "That sounds perfect. Beer, pumpkin carving, and maybe a pot of chili for dinner?"

Colorful vendor tents were scattered along the sidewalks of Washington Park, offering up the last of the season's crops; winter squash, potatoes, onions, peppers, and garlic. While Charles selected vegetables, Dani picked up some home baked bread and jam, and browsed handmade crafts, deciding on winter scarves for both of them.

A bright pink booth caught her attention, and she wandered over, smiling at the two women handing out brochures. "Have you registered for the American Pink Ribbon event next weekend?" One of the women offered her a registration form.

"I haven't." Dani glanced at the form, and noted the registration fee. "Do you have information on where the funds actually go?"

"Of course." The woman dug in a box sitting on the ground under the table. "We pride ourselves in promoting awareness, and funding mammograms and research."

Nodding politely, Dani remembered Honey's comment about awareness. "I'm more interested in the research. Have you heard that the Rush Institute has developed a vaccine to prevent breast cancer?"

The comment caught the attention of several people standing around the table and one of them spoke up. "Prevention? Is that true?"

A man in his mid-forties came over to join the conversation. "I want that for my wife. I'd take her anywhere in the world to get a vaccine to prevent her from getting breast cancer. She just lost her sister after a two-year fight. It was heart wrenching for the whole family, and now she's really scared. Do you have information on where she can be vaccinated?"

Several women waved their hands at her for information, and Dani gave the man a sympathetic look. "It's not actually available yet. It's been tested in mice with one hundred percent success. It's ready for clinical trials." She turned to the woman who handed her the brochure. "It needs funding for the FDA application process, and for manufacturing and conducting the study in women."

"I'm not aware of it, but I'd encourage them to submit a grant proposal. I'm sure it's something we would be interested in." The woman seemed to be sincere.

Dani tried to keep her voice steady. "They did submit a request for funding, and the foundation you represent denied the application." Dani knew it was a blunt statement, but it was the truth. Several people stood around the pretty pink kiosk looking confused.

The woman looked horrified, but quickly regained her composure. "There is a formal process, and perhaps some information was missing."

Two women handed in their registration forms and checks, and turned to Dani. "Where did you say this research is happening?"

"The Rush Institute, right here in Denver."

"How did you find out about this?" A small crowd was gathering now, and Dani watched most of them fill out registration forms, and hand over checks. *Don't they comprehend what I'm saying?*

"I work for the Tribune, and visited the lab almost a month ago. The research is impressive."

"I read that article! It's so sad that he died before his dream could be realized. I feel certain that this will be moved forward very quickly."

"Not without funding," Dani said.

A bouquet of orange Cosmos appeared in front of her, and she turned to see Charles and Terrell grinning. "Ready to carve some pumpkins?"

"Thank you, these are pretty." She accepted the flowers and held up a finger. "Yes, one sec."

Dani turned back to the people gathered around the booth. "Ladies, please look it up on the internet. The Rush Institute."

"You forgot your registration form!" One of the women in the booth called out to her.

"No, I didn't forget. I prefer to donate to preventing the disease, rather than funding more toxic drugs to use after I'm already sick." Dani waved. "Have a nice day, ladies."

Dani heard the screened door slam. "It smells great it

here!" Terrell hefted a big pumpkin on the kitchen island, and put a six-pack of beer in the refrigerator.

"Chili should be ready in about an hour. Charles is in the garage cleaning out an old chest to use for the Halloween candy. We've decided to be pirates this year. Are you planning to masquerade as the friendly neighborhood detective?" She teased.

"I'll be on call, as usual." He punched her gently on the arm, "So yeah, I'll be your friendly neighborhood detective well into the night."

Charles came in from the garage carrying the old wooden chest, which was now cleaner than he was. "Mmmmm, dinner smells good. I'm gonna take a quick shower."

Terrell opened two beers, handed one to Dani, and sat on a stool at the island. "How's life at the Trib, Dani-girl?"

"Dull in comparison to the research I'm doing on my own." She sat down beside him. "I'm beginning to believe these charity organizations have no intention of funding prevention. It would put them, and a lot of drug companies, out of business. I'm still researching, but I think you're right about one thing Terrell. Money is at the root of all evil."

"Had a taste of reality, did you? Nothing surprises me anymore." Terrell shook his head. "Not after eighteen years on the force. Once someone gets an taste of power, or money, all bets are off."

Dani got up to take a pan of blueberry muffins out of the oven. "I shouldn't be surprised—I do work at a newspaper. But, I'm usually involved in lifestyle pieces, and the more positive side of the news." She whipped lemon zest into butter and set it beside the plate of warm muffins, "Want one while they're warm?"

"You're gonna spoil me." Helping himself to a muffin, he rolled his eyes. "Mmm, mmm, mmm! There's not a bakery within a hundred miles of Denver that can bake like you, Dani-girl. You sure you didn't miss your calling?"

"Don't tempt me. I'm so wrapped up in this...this..." Dani waived her arm, and plopped down on her stool, sulking. "I can't even call it an investigation. I have no authority to delve into this, I can't use my credentials to get meaningful interviews, and I'm writing incognito. What kind of journalist does that?"

Grinning at her with a mouthful of muffin, he teased, "One who doesn't want to be busted for insubordination?"

"Who's insubordinate?" Charles grabbed a beer from the fridge, and scooted his stool behind Dani, wrapping his legs around hers.

"Your sneaky wife, that's who." Dani leaned back against his chest. "Terrell thinks I should hang it up in favor of chef's whites, and a toque."

Charles winked at Terrell. "I happen to know someone who can arrange financing for a bakery."

"All I'm saying is, a guy can't live on doughnuts alone."
Terrell dabbed up the last crumbs of muffin with his finger.

"I'm a woman of many talents," she said. "Just wait 'til you see the devilish patterns I made for those pumpkins."

Terrell laughed. "You sure scared up a crowd at the park today. Did you see how many people you attracted in just a few minutes? I gather you have a grudge against those nice ladies at the pink ribbon booth."

"No, I don't have anything against the ladies at the booth. I doubt they know what's going on right under their noses. It's just that I don't understand why some people are so hesitant to embrace the only real progress that's been made in decades. It's like they can't think for themselves, so they just follow whoever yells the loudest. Or in this case, the ones who have the most money for publicity."

"We do live in a capitalistic society." Charles said.

"I know. Money makes the world go 'round. But, this is health we're talking about, not the latest and greatest computer. I've been researching this for a month now, and it's simply not right that findings with so much promise are sitting on a shelf, while women continue to smile and hand over checks to the same foundations that have shown no real progress since the industry adopted that damn pink ribbon. It's like a club they're all loyal to, or something. Isn't Dr. Jennings' research worth a ten million dollar try?"

Terrell was thoughtful for a moment. "Jennings. I'm

tryin' to think why I know that name? Oh yeah, Suzanne Jennings. That's her late husband, isn't it? That family's had a rough year, what with his accident, and then that break-in."

"Break-in? Did someone break into the lab at Rush?" Dani straightened up, her senses sharpened.

"Here we go..." Charles rolled his eyes.

"Not that place. Rush is like Fort Knox. No one's gettin' through that security—at least not easily. No. Someone broke into his house—well his wife's house. Made off with a laptop, and a couple of boxes from the lab. It was reportedly all personal stuff, but Mrs. Jennings woke up, and scared the perp, before he could take much. Poor lady looked dog-tired, and the robbery really rattled her. Seemed like a nice lady, though."

"She's lovely. I met her briefly at the hospital the night her husband passed away." Dani said.

"Hey, don't you read your own paper, Dani-girl? These calls are always in the police report section."

"I used to read it cover to cover, but I don't pay much attention to the police report section since I know we have you keeping an eye out for our neighborhood. Did you ever catch the person who broke in?"

"No, not yet. I suspect the guy was wearing gloves—most burglars do. We ran prints through the system, but nothing came up, so we don't have a suspect yet."

Dani made mental notes, "When was this?"

"Shortly after her husband died. A week later, maybe."

Dani's instincts went on full alert. "Terrell, you said the burglar took boxes from the lab. Do you think those two incidents could be connected? Could someone have wanted to get to Dr. Jennings to sabotage his research?"

Terrell cocked his head. "The incidents seemed unrelated until now. I wasn't aware of the push back he was getting' on his research. And, since no one was hurt during the robbery, and they didn't take anything of great value, it hasn't been a top priority. It's a stretch, but if we can connect the robbery to the hit and run, the research could be a motive."

Charles put his arms around his wife. "Sweetheart, I'm not sure I want you involved in this. Will you please leave this to the professionals? Terrell has enough information to dig into now, but if the two of you are right, this could have enormous implications. Will you please ask Coop to assign this to one of the investigative reporters?"

"No way! This is my story. Coop has already shut it down, and unless I have concrete proof, he won't be interested anyway. I want to see this through myself."

She turned to Terrell, "Will you let me know if you find a connection when you check those files?"

"I'll have to be careful what I disclose about an ongoing investigation, but I can let you know if there *is* an investigation connecting the two."

Charles let out a long breath, "I pray they aren't

connected. Dani's wound up enough, as it is."

She could tell Charles was worried, but she couldn't let this go. Not now. Her head was spinning with possibilities. *How far would a charity go to protect it's own interests? Terrell is right, money is the root of all evil and...* Her heart was beating harder now. *Murder?*

# CHAPTER 18

Coop made his way through a pile of assignments and press releases. "The fire departments are handing out treats for Halloween this year, and requesting donations to the food bank. Got that covered, Driscoll?"

"Got it!"

"Oh, and Driscoll, take this press release." He shoved the page across the table. "Mona Davenport wants this announced during Breast Cancer Awareness Month. Can you have something ready for the morning edition?"

She nodded, and accepted the single sheet of paper, and read it to herself. *American Pink Ribbon Foundation announces plan to eradicate breast cancer in ten years. What?* Now she felt foolish about last night's conversation with Terrell. Charles was right; her imagination was out of control.

Coop walked by her cubicle after the meeting, and

motioned for her to follow him. When they reached his office he closed the door behind them.

"She asked for you specifically, or I'd have given it to Pete. I want this handled with the utmost care, Driscoll. Stick with the facts, understood?"

"Of course, Coop. Thanks for the opportunity. I wasn't sure you'd ever let me interview her again."

"You're right, I had no intention of putting the two of you in the same room. I assume this is a peace offering being extended to you."

"I guess." She was doubtful but wanted to keep the peace. "I'll go over there this morning."


Dani had been to the foundation offices before, and she was always impressed with how Mona had managed to use so much pink and make it look tasteful.

"Good morning, Jackie. Is Mona available by any chance?"

Jackie finished chewing, smiled, and nodded. "She is for you. She's very excited about this announcement; it's been top secret until today. She said I could release it to the local TV news in the morning, and to the rest of the country on Thursday. You're to have the initial interview."

"I'm honored, and excited to hear all about it." Now she could put all this research behind her, make a final blog entry, and get her life back.

Jackie started to get up, "Let me see if she's in her..."

"Dani, dear!" Mona appeared with a stack of folders, and set them down in front of Jackie. "So good of you to stop by."

"Jackie, please bring us coffee, and some of those lovely scones I picked up this morning." Holding a hand out to Dani, "Please come in, dear."

Dani followed Mona to her office. "Coop said you requested me, and I want to thank you for that, Mona. I'm anxious to hear about your newest project."

"Yes I did. You seemed so passionate about prevention the last time we chatted. I never thought to ask if breast cancer has touched your life. Your mother? A sister or close friend perhaps?"

"No, actually I've never known anyone with breast cancer. I've met them in passing, of course, but no one close to me. The research I've done on the subject is fascinating, though."

Jackie came in with a beautifully prepared tray of refreshments, complete with a small vase of pink sweetheart roses.

"The scones are from a new bakery a couple of blocks from here. They're simply delicious. I hope you'll do a feature article for them since we don't have many quality bakeries in Denver."

"I'll make a point of it." Dani nodded, and noted the

name of the bakery.

"I'm so glad you decided to get behind the research at Rush. They must be thrilled. Did you fund the entire project?"

Mona stopped dabbing the corners of her mouth with the pink linen napkin. "My dear, what do you mean?"

Dani's pencil was still poised over her notepad. "The news release you sent Coop. It says," unfolding the paper she'd tucked into the back of her notepad, "American Pink Ribbon Foundation announces plan to eradicate breast cancer in ten years." She turned to Mona, and narrowed her eyes. "I wasn't aware that anyone besides Rush was this close."

"Oh dear." Mona looked sympathetically at Dani. "I told you I would contact you if I found there was any hope of success at Rush. The lead researcher..."

"Yes, I know what you told me. The release you sent was hardly complete, though." *Calm down. You can't blow this; Coop will kill you.* Sitting back in in her chair, Dani smiled sweetly at Mona. "I'm sorry. I'm obviously confused. Why don't you tell me about your plans?" She settled back in her chair, forcing herself to listen with a reporter's ears, calmly and objectively.

"The audacity of that woman!" Dani stormed through the bullpen looking for Coop, and found him at Pete's cubicle. "Coop, when you have a minute."

She knew he could read her like a book; had been able

to since she was three years old. She'd never had the patience to hide her emotions like a Pulitzer Prize winning reporter, so it didn't surprise her that, when Coop came by her desk, all he had to say was, "My office."

She grabbed her notes, and walked briskly to his office, feeling as though her head could explode at any moment. She closed the door behind her, and sat down in front of his desk, taking a deep breath.

Coop looked annoyed. "What is it now, Driscoll?"

"Coop, Mona Davenport just told me she has plans to develop a vaccine to prevent breast cancer, and her goal is to have it done in ten years."

Coop sat behind his desk and shrugged his hands. "And that's a problem because...?"

*Does he really not see what I see?*

"It's a problem because it's redundant. Remember the prevention that already exists? The one she still refuses to fund? Coop, Rush has already developed a vaccine, and she's wasting precious years by starting over before we've tested its efficacy on women. For every day this vaccine goes unfunded," she referred to her notes, "Eight-hundred-ten women will be diagnosed and one hundred eight will die. In ten years' time that's almost three hundred ninety five thousand deaths and almost three million women who will be told they have this awful disease. Starting over is a waste of time, a waste of lives. You don't see the problem?"

"Driscoll, the projects Mona decides to fund, and the ones she doesn't fund, are not our business. Just write the piece I assigned you." Looking miserable, Coop opened his desk drawer, and fished out four Ibuprophen, swallowed them, and chewed up two antacids. "I don't want to have another discussion about this."

"That stuff will kill you one day, Coop." She calmed herself, not wanting to add to his headache, or his ulcer.

"Okay, I'll write up the press release. But really, that woman is a piece of work."

# CHAPTER 19

Terrell quickly flipped through the hit and run file, and snatched the photos of the '72 Coup Deville seen pulling out of a parking space, and running into Dr. Jennings. Several surveillance cameras captured the scene in the business district where the incident took place, leaving a clear concept of what occurred that night. What wasn't clear was whether the driver actually intended to hit a pedestrian. Or more important, whether he targeted Dr. Jennings.

Hit and runs were often difficult to solve. Many of these drivers didn't have a valid driver's license, some were in the country illegally, some were intoxicated or young, and a high percentage fled the scene because they were scared. In this case, the photos of the driver were fuzzy, making it hard to tell whether he, or she, was distracted, or intent on committing a crime.

Taking the best photos of the vehicle from the file, Terrell found his partner. "Collins, Let's go back to the Jennings neighborhood and talk to the neighbors again. I want to show these shots of the DeVille on the chance that one of them can ID it."

"Sure, any excuse to get out of here for a decent cup of coffee. You buying?"

"Yeah, I'll spring for the coffee. Grab the file."


Collins flipped through the file they'd put together the morning of the robbery at the Jennings residence. "Dolores. Dolores Burnett mentioned seeing a car parked in the street that night. Do you really think the hit and run and this robbery could be related?"

Terrell pulled the unmarked car over at the corner about a block from the Jennings residence. "I didn't until Dani stirred up the pot last night. Now my gut tells me there might be something here, and you know I always follow my gut."

"Um hum. I've seen you follow your gut. To the coffee shop, to the donut shop, to the hamburger joint." Collins finished her fast food breakfast sandwich, and started to get out of the car, "Want to start with Mrs. Jennings?"

"No. If nothing turns up I don't want to upset her by implying fowl play. That poor woman has been though enough already." Terrell said.

Working their way toward the Jennings residence, they

rang the doorbell of a stately colonial home with four tall columns gracing the front porch. The home was grand, but didn't blend in the neighborhood of Tudor and craftsman-style homes.

"Hey. I remember y'all." The stylish Dolores Burnett looked to be about thirty-two and, like the style of her home, was obviously rooted in the south. "How are you?"

"Hello Mrs. Burnett." Terrell checked the file and began. "When we talked last, you mentioned seeing a dark car parked in the street the night of the Jennings' break-in. Can you tell me, is this the car you saw?"

"Oh, Detectives please call me Dolores." she reached out and shook their hands. "Mrs. Burnett sounds like my mother-in-law, bless her heart, I love her but..." she turned her head toward a beeping sound inside the house. "Oh, that's mah oven. I'm bakin' a cake. D' y'all care to come in?"

After Dolores' cake was safely out of the oven, she invited them to sit down. "I poured us some fresh sweet tea.

Collins took one sip of the syrupy-sweet tea, and set the glass down. "We'd like you to look at these photos; see if you recognize this car." She handed Dolores a few photos of the DeVille.

Dolores's face lit up. "Mah Daddy had one a these. It's a Coup Deville. Prob'ly around," she bit her lip looking at the ceiling, "must've been 1972. Mama hated that car. Thought the neighbors would think us uppity, drivin' around in a

149

Cadillac, and all."

Terrell nodded, "That's right, this car is a '72 Coup Deville. Thinking back to the night of the Jennings' break-in, Dolores, you said you got up in the middle of the night, and noticed a car parked across the street. Could it have been this car?"

Dolores shuffled through the photos, and tapped her finger on one. "You know, I believe it could be. I woke up thirsty and was on my way downstairs for some sweet tea. I saw this car," she tapped her perfectly polished finger on the photo, "parked over yonder. I saw it out the winda above the front door when I was comin' down the stairs. It was dark and all but, yes I believe it *was* this car." She nodded. "It caught my attention 'cause I'd never seen an old car like that parked in this neighborhood before. At least not at night."

Dolores shook her head, clicking her tongue behind her front teeth, "Tsk, tsk, tsk. Mah, they sure don't take cara of this one, do they? Just look at all those dents, and scratches. I couldn't see those in the dark but a person should take better cara their things."

"Yes, they should. Thank you Dolores. You've been very helpful." Collins took the photos.

"Do y'all think you found out who broke into Suzanne's house then?"

"We're just following up on leads at this time. Please call us if you think of anything else." Terrell handed her a business card.

"I surely will. Bye, bye y'all!"

When they were seated in the patrol car, Terrell looked at his partner. "Holy crap!"


Snipes sauntered to the garage, then slowed, letting his hand glide along the front of the car. *Time ta move on ol' girl. I'll miss ya though.*

He wanted to take the Coup Deville for one last spin before he traded it on something more suitable. He already had a bundle of cash stashed. A few more jobs like this and he could drive north through the Rocky Mountains into Canada, just like he'd dreamed.

He'd been close to making that happen ten years ago until the garment factory shut down, and outsourced all the jobs overseas. He'd been well liked at the factory, and enjoyed driving the forklift, loading trucks that would deliver clothing all over the U.S. and Canada.

He once dreamed of moving to Florida, but when he took a week's vacation, and hitched a ride north with one of the drivers headed to Canada, he was hooked. The beauty of Banff, Lake Louise, and the majestic mountain backdrop made an impression he couldn't shake. He'd taped scenic post cards up in his locker, and on his fridge at home. He would save some money, relocate to Banff, and start a family. It had felt good to have his life planned out, and have something to look forward to.

Times were rough back then since so many were unemployed. And though he was frugal, the savings he'd worked so hard stash away for his trip were gone in under a year. He moved into a little shack in the mountains west of Fort Collins, and took any odd job he could find, finally turning to petty theft just to pay the weekly rent on his room, and buy a few groceries.

One snowy evening, hungry, and desperate about his situation, Snipes went into a fast food restaurant, and ordered a small meal that he paid for with the last of his loose change. He sat at a booth eating, and watching the three young workers—none of them could've been over eighteen or nineteen. Scarfing down the last of his fries he daydreamed about how easy it would be to walk up to the registers, and demand all the cash. It was getting late—they were busy mopping the dining area, cleaning the grill, and one young girl, a pretty blonde, tidied the counter, stocking straws and ketchup packets.

He would never forget how calm he felt when the last customer left, and he stuffed his hand in his jacket pocket, sticking out his finger to make it look like he had a gun. He walked up to the pretty blonde girl, and she asked sweetly if he wanted something else. He felt a sneer spread over his lips—he couldn't control it—and he shook his jacket pocket, and told her, "Yeah, an apple pie. And I want all the cash. Every register. I'll take that to go please."

Her mouth flew open, but nothing came out. She looked terrified, her eyes so wide open she reminded him of a cartoon. Trembling, she opened the registers, and did as he asked.

*This is so easy!*

They both turned, Snipes and the girl, when the door opened and in walked the sheriff.

"Daddy!" She dropped the bag she'd been filling with cash, and ran instinctively to the sheriff, who pushed her behind him and drew his weapon.

"What's going on here?" The sheriff squinted his eyes at the only stranger he saw. "Take your hands out of your pocket, slow and easy."

"Daddy, he has a gun!"

The sheriff moved his finger to the trigger of the semi-automatic pistol, clearly ready to shoot now, and ask questions later.

The other two workers had stopped what they were doing, their eyes darting between him, the Sheriff, and the cash now strewn on the floor.

"No!" Snipes shouted. "No, I don't have a gun, see?" He raised his hands, palms out. "I'm sorry, I don't know what I was thinking. I'll go home. You won't see me in here again."

He started for the door, but the sheriff held up his hand.

"You're right on one count. I won't see you in here again." He drew out handcuffs, and came toward Snipes, still pointing his pistol. "But, as for home, buddy you'll be making your home in a cell for a long while. On the floor, face down."

Snipes thought he might loose the meal he'd just eaten, but he did as he was told, and got down on the floor looking at the cash strewn around him.

"You have the right to remain silent..."

Snipes racked up two years in the pen, just because the local sheriff was picking up his teenage daughter after work on a snowy evening. Under the circumstances it was better than being hungry, and cold. He learned the hierarchy of prison life fast, and learned it well, making friends with inmates who'd led sordid lives, and committed a multitude of crimes from grand larceny to murder for hire. Snipes looked up to them, and got an education in crime. The experience hardened him. Never in his life had he expected to be a convicted criminal.

After two years he felt like he'd learned the ropes, and the biggest lesson he took with him when he left prison, was that crime could indeed pay. The second lesson he learned was never trust anyone. As long as no one knew what you were up to, there was no one to rat you out.

Now out in the field, as he liked to call it, Snipes knew

he'd bungled some of his jobs, but always managed to convince his various employers of his skills; touting some of the stories he's heard in the pen as his own. The people who hired him assumed he was a professional since he was an ex-con and he'd done time, giving him plenty of opportunity to hone his skills on the job.

Sometimes he thought maybe he wasn't the sharpest tool in the shed, but his plan to get to Banff and start a new life was planted firmly in his mind, and he wasn't giving up on it this time. He knew the fastest way to make enough money to get there was to hire himself out to people who didn't want to get their hands dirty. There was no shortage of work. There was always someone who needed help.

Every morning when he saw the post card of Lake Louise on his fridge he made a vow to himself. *This line of work stays here, in Colorado. Canada is a new chapter.*

He glanced at his palm where he'd written the address of the subject of his new assignment, and turned into the Washington Park neighborhood. "Keep an eye on that reporter," he'd been told. Keeping a watchful eye was one skill he'd honed very well in the pen. That was one place where you learned to watch your back at all times.

He drove past the house slowly, turned around at the next intersection, and parked across the street. He doubted anyone was home since it was ten in the morning, so he closed the door of the Coup Deville and walked around the house, noting door and window locations. *Nice place. Prob'ly a snooty bitch.*

Mature landscaping kept the house mostly obscured from the street but Snipes found a path along the north side of the house lined with evergreens that he could easily navigate later if he needed a closer look. Satisfied he knew the lay of the land well enough he set off to replace his well-loved Caddy.

Snipes drove past several dealerships before he pulled into a Chevy lot just to see what they had. *Gotta start somewhere.* He sauntered around the used car section looking for an SUV suitable for a trip through the Rocky Mountains. Peering in the window of a gray Ford Escape, he nodded. *Escape. That's exactly what I'm gonna do.* He tried the door, found it unlocked, and sat carefully in the front seat, hands on the steering wheel. *Baby you were meant for me.*

"Welcome to Romano Chevrolet. How may I help you today?"

He looked up, and standing before him was an angel with a smile so bright it could light up the sun. Her hair shimmered around her slim shoulders, and he knew without a doubt, she was the most beautiful thing he'd ever laid eyes on. Heart pounding, he took in a deep breath to calm himself, and cleared his throat, wanting to sound important. "I'm lookin' for somethin' that will handle good in the mountains."

"This is a nice choice. Do you live in the mountains?" She asked.

"Not anymore, but I plan to real soon." He stood up, and hesitantly stuck out his arm to shake her hand. "I'm planning a nice long trip."

She took his hand and shook it, warmly. "Sounds like fun. I'm Honey. Honey Romano."

"Al. Just call me Al."

"Short for Alan?"

"No." he felt blood rushing to he cheeks "Name's Alistair but no one 'cept my Mom ever called me that."

"Alistair's a great name. Unique, and sophisticated." She was smiling at him now, giving him chill bumps in eighty-five degree weather. She looked up at the clear blue sky, and said, "It's a beautiful day for a test drive. Shall I grab the keys and a temporary tag for you?"

"Yep, I'd love to take 'er for a spin."

"Lovely! Follow me inside, and I'll get a copy of your drivers license."

She took his license, disappeared around the corner, and returned with a young salesman in a suit. "Al, this is Zach. He'll be happy to help you today. If you need anything at all, let me know, okay?" She flashed that gorgeous smile again, turned, and left him with the suit.

Snipes smiled after her, even though his heart sank to the bottom of his stomach. He took the keys from Zach and trudged out the door.

# CHAPTER 20

Dani drove home that evening, conflicted, disgusted, and exhausted. Slowing down in front of Terrell's house, she craned her neck to see if his car was in the driveway. *Nope.*

Charles was pulling weeds in the flowerbeds, and stood up, stretching his back. "Hi Sweetheart."

She hugged him, and sat on a porch step. "How was your day? I didn't expect to see you doing yard work on a weekday."

"It might snow tomorrow, and I don't want weeds taking over in the spring. Why the glum look?"

"Charles, this story gets more bizarre every day. I went to interview Mona Davenport today, and found out she's... Oh, there's Terrell, I need to talk to him. I'll be right back."

He shook his head, "Ambushing him before he can get in the door?"

She grinned back at him and headed across the street. "What can I say? I'm on a mission."

"Terrell, hi!" She waved as he was getting out of his car. "Do you have a few minutes to talk?"

"Sure." Nodding toward her house, he said, "What's Charles up to? Let's let him in on our conversation." He led the way back to the Driscoll property.

She followed him back to her yard, shoulders slumping.

"Charles. I wanted you both to know that, after our conversation and a little digging around, Collins and I have reason to investigate the Jennings hit and run."

Charles brushed the dirt from the knees of his jeans, looking from Terrell, to Dani, then at Terrell again.

Terrell continued, "Understand that I don't mean to imply there is fowl play, but I think there is enough information to escalate the investigations of both the Jennings incidents."

Dani started to speak, but Terrell held up his hand and said. "I can't say any more than that."

"Yes, I understand, but I can." The thoughts in her head made her dizzy. "And I don't mean to implicate anyone, but I wanted to say that Mona Davenport requested me for an interview today. The piece will run in the morning paper, but I can tell you right now she's announcing the development of her own vaccine. One that will compete directly with the Jennings' research. I suspect she's just buying time. Starting over like this, will take them at least ten years before they reach the stage Dr. Jennings has already achieved."

Charles started to interrupt, but Dani held up a finger, and continued. "This announcement serves only one purpose as far as I'm concerned. It conveniently keeps her foundation in the limelight while delaying the obsolescence of her business. She'll raise millions, maybe even billions, from this announcement. It's disgusting."

She could see Charles clenching his jaw.

As soon as she finished talking, he jumped in. "Easy now. Be careful what you say, Sweetheart. Isn't it possible Mona's advisory board simply has a better idea?"

"Terrell, what does this mean, exactly?" Charles asked.

"It's too early to know for sure if these two cases are connected. I don't want to worry either of you unnecessarily, but I do want you to be aware and cautious."

Dani frowned, and nodded. "I understand. There's something else you should know. When I called the Jennings lab to follow up on their progress, I found out that a supporter of the American Pink Ribbon Foundation is working at the lab now."

Charles responded quickly, "They have plenty of supporters, that doesn't mean a thing."

Dani stood her ground. "Maybe it's coincidence, but what if I said she's related to Mona's personal assistant?"

Terrell raised his brow. "Whoa, whoa, whoa! Slow

down Dani-girl. Listen to me. I came over here because I wanted Charles to hear what I had to say. If these two incidents are connected, this has the potential of becoming a dangerous situation. One I don't want you involved in." His tone was stern; one she hadn't heard directed at her before.

"Ditto." Charles swallowed hard, "I admire your passion, but will you please leave this to Terrell now?"

She bit her lip, looked from Terrell to Charles, and drew in a long breath. "I hear both of you. Thanks for the update, Terrell. I need to get dinner started." She stalked toward the front door.

Terrell called after her, "I assure you, I heard every word you said."

She went straight to her blog. *I can't believe no one sees what I see. The world will know about this if it's the last thing I do.* She typed out a title for her post. *Appetite for Profit Thwarts Prevention.*


Chopping vegetables gave Dani something constructive to do with her anger the next evening. Every major news station gave full coverage to Mona's story like it was something new. "Why don't they realize it's already been done?"

"Talking to yourself?" Charles wrapped his arms around her, nuzzling her neck with his chin on her shoulder. "Should I be worried?"

Turning and waving the knife in her hand, she let out some frustration. "This is sickening! The press is kissing up to her because she has money, power, and influence. The way they're responding, you'd think she owned the disease."

"Whoa!" Charles gently took the knife from her, setting it on the counter. "Careful with that knife."

"As Honey pointed out, all this publicity she generates is solely for the purpose of raising millions of dollars, which she spends on more awareness campaigns, which nets her even more publicity, adding millions more to her coffers. You wanna know what I think?"

"What do you think, Sweetheart?" Charles put on the kettle for tea.

"That woman has no more intention of finding a prevention for breast cancer than the Pope has for funding a world wide distribution of condoms!"

The expression on his face disarmed her, and she stopped, and laughed at herself. "I know I'm on my soapbox again. But, Charles why is the press so keen on giving her all this free publicity while the Rush vaccine can't even get a ten second mention? It's *news*! They're *journalists*!"

"Reputation." He rubbed her back, soothingly. "She has a long history of doing this, everyone knows about her, which means people will listen when she speaks."

Dani looked at him thoughtfully. "Do you really think that's all it is, Charles?"

"I really do." He poured hot water into teacups while she stir-fried veggies.

"Okay, that makes sense but it doesn't explain why she's doing this now. Why she's starting a project from scratch that already exists, and thus far has proven to be a near perfect success."

"It's true, Rush published its success, but no one knows if it will work on women. They only know it works on mice." He pulled out plates and cups and set the kitchen table.

She sighed, tired of hearing this line of reasoning. "Her vaccine, if she ever really develops it, will be in the exact same situation as the Rush vaccine is now, because it has to be tested on mice first, no matter who develops it. But the sad thing is, millions more women will endure chemotherapy and mastectomy, many more will die, while we wait ten more years for Mona's research to get to the same stage as the Rush vaccine is now. In my opinion, there's something very wrong about that." She shook her head and went back to her veggies.

Later that evening, Dani logged onto Hope Incorporated. She found a few typical comments from outraged women vowing to support the Rush research, but one in particular stood out. It had been posted about half an hour ago. "Interesting post. Want to know more?" She raised her eyebrows, clicked the link, and her fingers froze over the keyboard. Her heart began to beat so hard in her chest she could feel it pulsing in her head. She stared at the solid pink page displaying a single line of bold, black text across her screen.

"I know who you are."

With a shaking hand she scrolled up and down the page but there was nothing else there. Unnerved, Dani closed the browser, and her laptop, and sat there, trying to calm the pounding in her chest. But, curiosity got the better of her, so she logged into her blog again. The anonymous comment was the most recent comment displayed. She clicked on the link again, and her mouth went dry when she read, "Site not found." *What?* She tried again, but the link was broken.

She answered some other comments, wrote a short post, and scrolled down to examine the comment again. It was gone. Scrolling up and down, she searched but the strange comment that had been there just minutes before, had vanished into the ether. *Was I hallucinating?*

She sat back with a sigh, wondering what she was doing. How many different ways could she say the same thing and hope for a different outcome? *This is madness. Maybe Charles is right; it isn't my problem. Maybe I should just let it go.*

# CHAPTER 21

Dozens of women wearing pink headscarves stared at her from reclining chairs. They were pale, and appeared to be sick. Their eyes were devoid of eyelashes, and eyebrows. Plastic IV tubing protruded from their chests, and fiery-red liquid raced to their veins. They looked so weak, so tired.

Some were crawling on the floor, dragging IV poles, and vomiting into waste cans. Others passed around baskets heaped with pink headscarves. Industrial-sized bottles of Pepto Bismol, and boxes of saltine crackers lined a countertop.

Out of the corner of her eye she saw Mona at the end of a long hallway, eyes fixed on her, moving slowly, and intently closer. She was rolling an IV pole, the floor blistering behind her from toxic liquid dripping from a dangling needle. *Sssst.*

"No! Stay away from me," Dani cried defiantly, her muscles tightening.

One by one, more women crowded into the room. They reached out to her, their faces contorted with anguish, begging for help.

"What can I do? Please tell me!" Dani cried out to them.

Hundreds of women filled the room, and lined the impossibly long hallway.

*Sssst.*

They turned in unison toward Mona, whose eyes were fixed on Dani, as she moved closer, closer, closer. Their hair turned to pink ribbons as she passed them. Silent tears streamed down their faces. They seemed transfixed by Mona.

*Sssst. Sssst.*

The sound of the liquid searing the floor grew louder as Dani backed away, but in an instant Mona was on her, backing her into a reclining chair. *Sssst.* Mona pulled a long pink ribbon from her diamond broach, intent on her next victim. She swiftly strapped Dani's arm to the chair, pushed her back to a reclining position, picked up the dripping needle, and aimed at a vein.

"Stay away from me! Stop!" Dani flailed around desperately, but Mona had her firmly pinned down. Her chest heaved with the sickening stench of panic, but still she couldn't get enough air. "Don't touch me! Nooooo!"

She felt a warm hand on her shoulder, and Dani bolted straight up in bed. Her pajamas were wet with sweat. Her entire body trembled, and her chest felt like it would explode under the pressure of her pounding heart.

Charles reached over, and pulled her down beside him, wrapped her in his arms. "Sweetheart, it's just a dream." Stroking her hair, he whispered, "Breathe now. Shhhhhh, shhhhhhh, you're all right. Look around you. You're at home, with me."

Dani jerked from his embrace, and sat up stick-straight on the side of the bed. Her voice quivered, "I can't lay down, Charles I have to get up. I can't go back to that dream. It was horrible. Evil."

"Okay, I understand. Let's go downstairs and make some tea." Charles helped her into a dry t-shirt, draped a robe over her shoulders, and took her hand. "Come on, Sweetheart."

Dani hadn't said another word and, despite the thick robe wrapped around her, she was still trembling. She thought she saw something move outside the kitchen window, but it was too dark to see anything.

Charles handed her a cup of tea. "Do you want to tell me about your dream?"

She tried several times to verbalize the dream, explain the terror she felt, but mercifully it was slipping away. What remained in her consciousness didn't make sense—even to her.

"Sweetheart, this is stress coming out. You need to let go of this story. Let someone else dig into it. Remember, you said the reason you weren't an investigative reporter was because of the hours involved. You said you wanted a personal life, and children someday."

She looked at him with eyes full of sadness. "I know. That's true, but I can't let go of this." Shaking her head, and shrugging her shoulders, "I just can't."

"Dani look," he reached across the breakfast table, and squeezed her hand, "if this is such a big story, surely someone will cover it. It isn't your responsibility, and I'm concerned about the way it's affecting you."

She shook her head. "I don't know whether anyone's covering it anywhere. My instincts tell me I need to dig in, find out why everyone seems to want to sweep this under the carpet. And Mona... What about this makes her so angry? Do you think she's jealous?"

"Jealous? I guess I'm not following. Mona Davenport isn't a scientist. Why should she be jealous?"

Dani felt flustered. "That's not the right word. I can't quite put my finger on it. Maybe she wants to be the one responsible for developing the ultimate cure, which in this case is a prevention. But, she could just as easily be the one who funded it, and everyone would win."

"Sweetheart, she's not a researcher, and I don't' see what difference you can make at this point. Coop has rejected the idea of more articles on the Jennings research."

Lowering her head, she sipped her tea thoughtfully. "Yes, but he doesn't own my personal time, does he?"

He gently tipped up her chin, "No, he doesn't. But, do you really think you can make a big enough impact with a blog?"

"I don't know." She stared out the window, "Probably not. I just know I have to solve this for my own peace of mind." She shifted her focus to his sweet face, and warmed her hands with her teacup. "No, it's more than that. Women deserve to know about this, and the research deserves to be funded. Can you imagine if this vaccine is as effective on women as it is on mice?"

She searched his eyes for understanding. "I have to find a way to get the Rush story the attention it deserves."

# CHAPTER 22

Dani was exhausted after the night of fitful dreams. A brief phone call told her Honey was working at the Chevrolet dealership. *Maybe I can chat with Honey while I get my car winterized.*

"Good morning. It's good to see you, Dani." Honey strode toward her, arms outstretched, and welcomed her with a hug. "I've been thinking about you since I read your article on Mona's funding for an alternative vaccine. Very well done, even if I was seething as I read it."

Dani laughed. "I was seething as I wrote it. Do you know, Mona actually requested me for that article?"

Honey shook her head. "I've come to realize there is a grand plan behind everything that woman does. I still haven't given up hope that Rush can get their research funded."

"Then you still believe in the Rush vaccine?"

They strolled around the lot together, and Honey continued. "Of course I do. It's the most promising research I've seen anywhere, and believe me, I've looked." Honey flashed her famous smile. "Actually, I've been up to something. After our last chat I called Seth McCleary at the lab. He's been a part of the research team for a long time, and I have complete confidence in him. They continue to show 100% prevention in three mouse models."

"I'm giving some thought to starting my own campaign on their behalf." Honey beamed. "I have my marketing department working on ideas to get all my dealerships involved. If we can move this forward, it could be available in time for my daughters."

"That's wonderful, Honey. But, why do you think they can't get any real traction for awareness and funding? It's a mystery to me because most women are enthusiastic when they hear about this. They're hopeful, and impressed, but then those same women turn around and donate to the same tired programs that have made no meaningful progress in decades."

Honey nodded. "I know. I don't understand that either. I wonder if they realize that if they don't give this vaccine a chance, their children and grandchildren will be funding the same awareness campaigns we're funding today. There's no end to breast cancer without a change in the way we approach it."

Dani agreed. "I don't know why this has such a hold on me. It obviously has your attention too, Honey. Why?"

"Because the risk factors are so diverse they add up to nothing except to prove that if you're a woman, you're at risk. It tells me no one really knows what the risk factors are, except gender, and even men can get breast cancer. A virus, and the ability to turn it off via a vaccine, makes perfectly good sense to me. Why should it be viewed any differently than the HPV vaccine? "

Dani admired Honey's way of maintaining her composure. "I wish I could figure out how to balance my emotions the way you do. You always seem to be relaxed, and happy. How do you do it?"

"It's something I learned when I was going through treatment. I knew I had to steady my emotions to give my body the best chance of recovering. More importantly, I wanted to maintain a peaceful home life, and sense normalcy for my girls. I learned to let go of things I couldn't change. It stuck."

Honey paused for a second. "And Dani, I appreciate the fact that you are so easy to talk to. I don't typically open up to anyone about this."

"How are your adorable little girls, by the way? And what brings you to the Chevy dealership today when you have such a gorgeous office at the import lot?"

Honey pointed to an old beater parked around the side

of the building, "Paperwork. A customer traded that in yesterday, and paid cash for the SUV he bought. Not a check, not even a debit card...cash. It causes extra paper work. I have to report anything over ten thousand dollars cash to the IRS. It happens so infrequently at these dealerships that I typically handle the paperwork myself."

"Looks like whomever it was needed a new car. That one's pretty old, not to mention being a polluting, gas-guzzler."

Honey agreed. "The Escape he bought will save him a bundle on gas."

"What will you do with that old clunker? I hope it doesn't end up on the road again."

"The De Ville will go to the junk yard, and likely be parted out. Amazingly, it does run."

"That's as good a way to recycle an old car as any, I guess." She pulled the vibrating cell phone out of her pocket. "Oh, car is finished, and I should let you get back to your paperwork. Thanks for taking the time to chat with me, Honey. And, give me a call when your campaign is ready, I'd love to write up an article to give it an extra push."

"I'll take you up on that!" Honey turned, and waved.

Snipes parked his new ride a few houses away from the reporter's house, and checked the clock on the dash when she pulled her car into the driveway.

"Time to turn up the volume on this little drama." He watched her bound up the porch steps, and unlock the front door.

"Enjoy your evening, little miss snooty bitch. Tomorrow's gonna be a wild ride." His upper lip curled into a sneer. *Apparently, you pissed off the wrong person, Missy.*

# CHAPTER 23

Dani mulled over her last conversation with Mona, and her chat with Honey. She pulled out of the rainy driveway, glancing in her rear view mirror in time to see a gray SUV pulling away from the curb, continuing in her direction. *Have I seen that car before?*

She shrugged, turned up the radio, and stopped at a red light where a crossing guard was helping children cross the street in front of the elementary school. Going over the details of the investigation in her head, she noticed the driver of the gray vehicle pulling his cap lower, almost covering his eyes. But, when the light turned green he made a left turn behind her. *Probably lives somewhere in the neighborhood.*

The rain turned to slush, and Dani wondered which of her colleagues had guessed today's date for the first snowfall in the office pool. She drove another three blocks, waited for the light to turn green, and pulled into the intersection. A horn blasted a long warning.

She started to break, but the car behind her was in a skid, trying to stop. An engine revved, and for a split second she saw an SUV careening straight toward her.

"Watch where you're going!" Dani called out to the oncoming car pushing her horn in warning.

Braking hard, she turned the steering wheel toward the curb to avoid hitting the Escape in her path. She cried out when she saw two children in raincoats holding hands on the sidewalk–their eyes wide, and mouths open in shrill screams. The trajectory of the oncoming car was head on with hers, but the children were standing directly in the path of her safety.

Horrified, she whipped the steering wheel away from the children, and bracing for impact, slammed on her brakes. But her car didn't respond as she expected; it slowed only slightly. The gray SUV corrected at the last minute, and passed by her with only a fraction of an inch to spare. She could see his eyes were still hidden by the baseball cap, but his mouth was set in a contemptuous smirk as he passed within inches of her.

Chills ran through her when he gunned the engine, and kept going. She felt as if her heart would surely beat out of her chest, as she struggled to control the car, searching out the children, praying for their safety. The car behind her was unable to stop. It plowed into the back of her, sending her in a spinning motion toward the curb. Her gaze was fixed on the children, still holding hands, stuck like little statues to the sidewalk. The airbag burst open, then consciousness gave in to darkness.

Charles left the house five minutes after his wife, and heard sirens blasting through the rainy morning. Strobe lights flashed ahead in the distance. His route became a bottleneck as Denver police officers directed traffic along the only lane not blocked by emergency vehicles, and pedestrians.

It wasn't until he drove close by the ambulance that he recognized the wreckage was his wife's vehicle.

He pulled off the road, and ran toward the awful scene. He could see his wife slumped in the front seat, held in place only by the seatbelt. The airbag had deployed, and lay deflating over the front of her. He was running as fast as he could, fixated on the paramedics who were securing a collar around her neck. He dashed between pedestrians, the scene seemed impossibly far away. Paramedics eased her out of the car, onto a stretcher.

"Dani! Dani!" Frantic, Charles sprinted the last few yards, and latched onto one of the paramedics. "Is she all right?"

"Do you know who she is?" The paramedic pried his arm loose from Charles' grip. "I need you to let me work."

Charles hurried to the stretcher carrying his wife to the

back of an ambulance, and grabbed her hand.

One of the paramedics was talking to him. "What's your name, sir?"

"What?" Trying to make sense of what he was seeing and hearing made him dizzy, and he steadied himself on the arm of the paramedic.

"Sir, is she your wife?"

Charles forced himself to hold the paramedic's gaze. "Yes, she's my wife. Dani, Dani Driscoll. She's a reporter at the Tribune. She was just going to work." He looked at the paramedic with wide eyes as if that information might change the horrible scene in front of him.

"Sir… Mr. Driscoll, does your wife have any conditions we should be aware of?"

"Conditions? No, she's healthy, twenty-nine years old." Charles asked a series of rapid-fire questions. "Is she okay? Can she hear me? Why doesn't she answer me? Oh my God, is her neck broken?" He pressed his hands to his stomach.

"The neck brace is a standard precaution, not necessarily an indication of an injury. She is unconscious, though."

His knees threatened to buckled, but he forced them to hold. "Dani, talk to me, please!"

"Sir, we need to load her into the ambulance now. You can ride up front if you want to go with us to the hospital."

"Hospital? Yes, yes I'm going with her."

Someone handed him her satchel, closed the ambulance door, and the piercing sound of the siren followed them all the way to the hospital.

Snipes pulled his car to the back of the bowling alley where his employer was already waiting. He was still on a high from this morning's job. It was too bad he'd be giving up his life of crime once he reached Banff. He'd become good at disconnecting himself from people, and focusing only on the job at hand. He credited his success to lessons learned when he was broke, and hungry, after the plant closed. Now he enjoyed the challenge of each assignment, thinking, and planning for himself.

"Tell me you didn't drive that car this morning." His employer shoved a thick envelope into his hand.

"Yeah, I did. But I didn't hit her with it. I'm a good driver. Did I tell you I used to drive a forklift? I can maneuver a car like nobody's business." He stuffed the envelope into the front pocket of his jeans, trusting he didn't need to count it this time.

"Idiot! There were witnesses! And children close by for heaven's sake. Do I have to spell out every little detail? You said you were a professional."

"Two years in the pen, and you'd be a professional, too. I don't see the problem. I picked this car 'cause it blends in." *Always bitching about somethin', aren't you?* "Don't worry! See," he pointed to the back of the car, "no tags yet, and I moved outta the old neighborhood last night. Everything's under control."

"It better be. I can't be connected to you–*ever*. Not in any way–even if you're caught. You're paid very well to complete the tasks given to you, and if there are consequences to your actions, then the consequences are yours. Do we understand each other?"

"Yeah, yeah, yeah. You said to put a scare in 'er and I did." He was proud of this job, he was getting better and better at this. His new vehicle didn't have a scratch on it.

"Continue to keep an eye on her. Let me know as soon as she's out of the hospital, and use that cell phone I gave you to report anything unusual. By that I mean she goes to work, maybe the grocery store or salon, and back home again. Any other trips and I want to know about it, immediately. Are we clear?"

"Yeah, we're clear." Snipes hesitated only a moment before giving a nod and adding, "I'll need a weekly drop for surveillance. She's a reporter, that could mean a lot of gas for my new baby." He patted the hood, and winked, "Same price, see you here next week."

Snipes caught a glimpse of the narrowed eyes shooting daggers at him. He slipped into his car, turned up the radio and drove off, pounding the steering wheel to the beat of the song that was playing. *Yeah! Who's in charge now? Alistair*

The paramedics bypassed the emergency room admissions desk, and wheeled Dani straight to a private exam room.

"Knows who I am," she whispered, "Knows who I..."

The paramedic who was arranging her IV on the pole beside the hospital gurney looked at Charles. "She said that over, and over, in the back of the ambulance. Do you know what she means?"

"Knows who I am, knows who..." Her eyes fluttered. She winced.

Charles leaned in to hear her weak whispers, and shook his head, trying to come up with an explanation. "No idea."

Her left arm was splinted, and her right arm had an IV running in it, so gently stroked her cheek with his fingers, cringing at her bruised, and swollen face.

"Could just be a song stuck in her head. Something playing on the radio at the time of the crash maybe." He finished packing up his gear, and reached over to shake Charles's hand. "I think she'll be fine, Mr. Driscoll. Though I'm sure her left arm is broken. She's in good hands now."

Charles eyed the splint and prayed that was the worst of her injuries.

The nurse finished taking her vitals, and handed

Charles a clipboard. "Can you fill this out, please? I'll take it to the front desk when you've finished, but now I need to take her for some x-rays."

He finished the forms, and began to pace. *What's taking so long?* He looked at his watch–they'd been gone almost forty-five minutes.

He walked out into the hall in time to see two nurses wheeling her back. The first thing he noticed was her eyes were open and the cervical collar had been removed. *Thank God.*

He smiled, and leaned over to kiss her. As soon as they had her settled he grabbed her hand and stroked it. "Hi Sweetheart. How do you feel?"

Her voice was no more than a whisper. "Headache. Groggy. They said you were waiting for me." She was struggling to get the words out, and her lips quivered. "I was so scared. I almost hit two little children. Are they all right?"

In the commotion he hadn't seen any children, but she was the only one who'd left in an ambulance. "Yes, the children are fine. I was scared too, when I recognized your car. Do you remember what happened?"

"Um…" She licked her lips. "Things are a bit fuzzy. I remember those two little children holding hands, and screaming. I don't think I'll ever forget their terrified faces. Oh, Charles, what if…" She started to bring her hands to her face, and looked at the splint on her left arm.

"I remember hearing a horn, and tires screeching. Then..." She shook her head. "What did I hit? Is anyone else hurt?"

"I don't think anyone else was hurt, at least you were the only one who left the scene in an ambulance. Do you remember the ambulance?"

She grimaced. "No, I... The next thing I remember is the x-ray department. They had to lift me to the x-ray table. I was too dizzy to stand up."

Charles rubbed her hand. "It's okay, you'll probably remember eventually. You were hit from behind, and pushed into the electrical pole at the crosswalk. It must have been a horrendous impact. I'm so relieved you're okay."

He paused for a moment, not wanting to upset her. "Sweetheart, you kept mumbling something over, and over. Do you remember?"

She still looked confused. "No, what did I say?"

"You kept repeating something that sounded like, "Knows who I am." Does that mean anything to you?"

The doctor came in then, flipping through lab reports. "Mrs. Driscoll, I'm sorry we're meeting under these circumstances. I'm a fan of your column. Always so upbeat."

She smiled, then grimaced. "Thanks. I have a headache."

The doctor nodded. "Yes, I suspect you do. Those air bags pack a colossal punch. I'll order some pain meds for your

IV while they set that broken arm. We often see these kinds of injuries from airbag deployment."

Charles nodded. "Is she okay, otherwise? No internal injuries?"

"She has significant bruising of the chest and ribs. She'll be sore for several weeks. I want to admit her for overnight observation, just to make sure nothing else comes up."

Charles agreed. "Whatever she needs. I don't want to take any chances."

A nurse came in and requested the doctor's assistance with another patient, and he turned to Dani before he left. "Someone will be in to set that arm in a few minutes. Do you have any other questions?"

"No, I'm fine. Thank you doctor."

Dani looked up at her husband, tears silently streaming into her hair. "I sure made a mess of this day, didn't I?"

He bent down, and kissed her. "All that matters is you're okay."


As soon as she was settled into a private room she asked for a phone. "I need to call Coop. He's probably wondering why I didn't show up this morning."

"I called him while they had you in x-ray, but he'd probably like an update. Want me to call him?" Charles pulled his cell phone from his pocket, and grinned, pointing to the fresh cast on her left arm. "Looks like you're going to learn to manage with one hand for awhile."

She looked at the cast, shrugging, "It could be worse. At least it's not my right hand. I'll call, and fill him in so he won't worry." Her eyes focused off in the distance for a moment. "Actually, my head still hurts. Would you mind making a coffee run?"

"Sure. Would you like anything else?" He looked at his watch. "It's way past lunchtime. Why don't I go downstairs, and see what they're serving in the cafeteria?"

"That would be great. You're so good to me, Charles." She gave him a tired smile.

As soon as he was out of earshot she dialed. "Terrell, it's Dani. How did you hear about...? I'm fine; they're just watching me overnight. I want to talk to you, though, and I don't want to worry Charles. That would be great. I'll call you later when he leaves the hospital."


Coop and Charles arrived together, Coop with a huge vase of Rembrandt daisies, and Charles with her satchel hanging from his shoulder, and balancing two cups of coffee, and sandwiches.

"I sent out an email to the staff. They all send their best." Coop kissed her forehead. "It looks like you'll need some time off."

"Thank you for the flowers, Coop. You didn't need to

come all the way over here, though. I'm fine."

He chuckled, looking around at the IV, and monitors attached to her in various places. "Yes, I can see that." Coop made himself comfortable in a chair by the window, and watched her scarf down her sandwich.

"What?" She looked at her boss, and long time friend, taking another big bite. "I'm hungry. Car accidents take a lot out of a person." She started to laugh, but grimaced instead. "My chest is sore. I have a bruise in the exact pattern of a seatbelt."

Coop stood up. "The next few days will probably be worse. Take the rest of the week off, and don't worry about your assignments. I'll send Pete to Mona's big press conference."

She pursed her lips.

Coop put a hand on Charles' shoulder. "Take care of our girl, and call me if you need anything at all."

When Coop was gone Charles cleared her tray, and filled the large water container. "What else can I get you, Sweetheart?"

"Sleep. I'm tired all of a sudden. It's probably from the meal on top of pain meds. Why don't you go to the bank and let me sleep, Charles? The nurses here are great; they'll take care of me." She yawned, sinking down into the hospital bed.

He rifled through her satchel, pulled out her cell phone, and put it beside her bed. "Okay, I'll let you sleep, but

I'll be back in a couple of hours. Call if you need anything. I'm only ten minutes away."

He kissed her tenderly. "I love you, Dani. You gave me an awful scare today."

"I love you, too Charles. Night night."

When she heard the elevator bell chime she grasped her cellphone, and dialed with her thumb. "Hi Maggie, it's Dani. Yes, Coop was just here, and he told me. I'll be fine, I'm just a little banged up. Listen, can you do me a favor? On my desk is an invitation from the Pink Ribbon Foundation that I won't be able to use. Can you please courier that over to Dr. Seth McCleary at the Rush Institute? Yes, it needs to go today–as soon as possible. Thank you Maggie, I'll see you in a few days."

*One more phone call then a nap.*

"Terrell, hi. Oh, just a broken arm and some bruises. I'll be fine. Hey, what kind of car did you say was involved in the Jennings accident?"

"No reason, I was just curious and I didn't want Charles to worry about me. A Cadillac De Ville? Thanks Terrell. I will. See you soon."

She tossed fitfully, trying to piece together the details of the accident. Muddled images played over, and over in her dreams. The faces of the children she'd come so close to running over, tugged at her heart. They looked so scared. Blaring horns sounded in her dreams. A sneering man in a baseball cap, a policeman taking notes, the strange comment on her blog. Charles leaning over her, demanding, "Who knows you, Dani, who knows you?"

*Who knows?* She woke herself up with a gasp. "Mona! Mona knows."

The painful gasp cut deep in her chest. She pushed the button that raised the head of her hospital bed, giving her the help she needed to sit up. She managed to swing her legs over the side of the bed holding her chest with her right arm.

She knew the best way to clear her head was to get her feelings written down. The cast was awkward, and she used it to hold her notepad steady on the over-bed table, while she worked to record her thoughts before they faded away.

*Okay, what do I actually know? The lead researcher at Rush was hit by a car and later died. Mona won't fund the vaccine at Rush but now she's announced the development of a new vaccine to do the same thing, but not for another ten years. Mona found a grant writer for Rush. But why would she help them? Is Keri a plant? A spy?* Dani tapped her pencil on the table.

*Oh, and the Jennings residence was broken into. Was it random? What were they after?* Her thoughts came so fast she was afraid she'd forget something before she recorded them to paper. *Someone has figured out Hope Incorporated is my blog, and...*

She looked back over her notes; her heart began to race. *No!*

Panic shot through her stomach in a wave of nausea. *A Cadillac De Ville hit Dr. Jennings.* She started scribbling furiously, remembering something Terrell had mentioned in passing. *Honey said the old beater on her lot was a De Ville that someone traded in. That person used cash to replace it.* "An Escape! I'm sure that's what she said."

She felt the blood drain from her face as she wrote with a shaking hand. *The SUV that caused my accident was a gray Escape. I'm sure of it. Mona knows I'm the blogger.*

A nurse rushed into her room. "Is everything okay, hon? Do you need something for pain?"

"Pain?" She turned to the nurse, confused.

"Your heart is racing on the monitor, and your blood pressure is up quite a bit." The nurse checked the monitor leads.

Dani looked up at her weakly, tucking the notepad under the sheet. "I'm fine, I was just... I had a bad dream."

"Accidents can do that to us, hon. Are you sure you're not in pain? Your doctor left orders for pain meds, as needed." The nursed helped her lie back, adjusted her bed, and filled her water container.

Dani reassured the nurse, "No, I'm fine now. Thank you."

As soon as she was alone she pulled out her notes, and

re-read them. *Would Mona actually let thousands of women die of breast cancer rather than have her foundation become obsolete?*

# CHAPTER 24

Reporters, photographers, and VIP's milled around the Diaxler Pharmaceuticals auditorium in anticipation of the press conference, and ceremonial cutting of an enormous pink ribbon.

Mona headed to the curtained-off area behind the stage that had been built especially for this event. She greeted ten little girls, each of who had each been given a gift certificate to buy a pink outfit of their choosing.

"You all look adorable!" She spun each of them around like princesses. "Does everyone know what to do? Are you all ready for the launch?"

They bounced, and giggled, and nodded their heads. "Yes!"

Mona clapped her hands together. "Wonderful! We'll start in a few minutes, and afterwards we have pink cupcakes, and pink lemonade, for everyone. Now, who needs to go to the bathroom?"

Several of them raised their hands, and Mona nodded to their mothers, smiling. "We'll bring them out in about half an hour. Thank you for your participation."

She spotted Todd going over last minute details of the press packets with his marketing team. After a quick scan of the area, Mona made a beeline to extend a personal greeting to Senator Newman, who'd just entered the conference room.

"Senator! Mingling with the press, I see." She pulled a check out of her jacket pocket, and tucked it into his.

He hugged her. "I'm here for the ribbon cutting ceremony actually, and I wanted to congratulate you on this marvelous new endeavor. Who better to liberate the world from breast cancer than it's most ardent warrior?"

"You're too kind, Senator. This was, of course, the doing of my advisory board. They're brilliant. Each and every one of them."

Todd joined them, and passed the Senator an envelope in a handshake. "Good of you to come, Senator Newman. I want you to know Diaxler is one hundred percent behind your re-election. There's a little something in there for your friends at the FDA as well. We hope to be first in line for approval when we're ready."

The Senator discretely tucked the envelope into his jacket. "It's an honor to be here for an event that will surely go down in history."

Todd extended his arm to Mona. "Shall we get this circus started?"

She straightened her tailored pink jacket, touched her trademark broach, and took his arm. "I do love a good circus."

Seth found two empty seats near the back of the auditorium. "I'm glad you could come with me on such short notice, Amy. Do you think she'll recognize us?"

"I think she's too busy to notice." Amy smoothed her hair, and looked around. "There she is, don't turn around. Look at me." Amy watched Mona talking to the Senator. "She's schmoozing with Senator Newman. Where did you say you got these invitations?"

"The reporter from the Denver Tribune sent them by courier late yesterday afternoon. The note said she couldn't attend, but she thought we might want to. I feel like a spy."

"Double-oh-Seth." She beamed up at him. "You look the part in that suit. Add some sunglasses, and Hollywood will be calling."

"Fat chance. Hey, there's a crowd around that table. Will you go see what that's about?"

"Sure"

Amy slid back into the chair beside him, grasping a press packet. "No one was checking, so I grabbed this. Oh, they're about to begin." She settled back in her chair.

After everyone was seated, Diaxler Pharmaceutical's Director of Marketing thanked everyone for coming, and introduced an impressive lineup of speakers. The CEO spoke about the dream of a world without breast cancer. Their new lead researcher, Dr. Hans Sauer, went on about his suspicion that a virus causes the disease.

Seth and Amy exchanged glances when Dr. Sauer was introduced, and Seth tightened his fists, mouthing "What?"

He leaned over and whispered to Amy. "How can they stand up there and talk like this is their idea? Like it's never been done before?"

Amy pressed her finger to her lips. "Shhhh."

V.P of Sales Todd Hastings spoke a few words of praise for the new research team, and then handed the microphone over to a beaming Mona Davenport.

"Ladies and Gentlemen, members of the press, it's an honor to be part of this innovative new program. With your help," she waved her arm across the room, "I am confident we will soon have the funding needed to carry this groundbreaking research through to it's end goal. Prevention."

"You know..." she paused for effect, walking across the stage, "it's been my life's work, since loosing my dear mother to this horrendous disease, to find a cure. My friends here at

Diaxler Pharmaceuticals have worked diligently for decades, developing life saving chemotherapies, and adjuvant therapies, to stop cancer in its tracks. Their achievements have been plentiful. Countless lives have been saved. But the last step... The most humanitarian step... Has eluded us."

Mona pulled a pink handkerchief from her jacket, dabbed the corners of her eyes, and whispered, "Until now."

She continued. "Until one brave scientist," she motioned to Dr. Sauer, "dared to throw out all traditionally accepted approaches," she lowered her voice, "and begin anew."

Mona paced back and forth across the stage. "As you can imagine, when my advisory board became aware of this extraordinary, paradigm changing research, we knew we had found the hope we'd only dared to dream of."

She nodded toward the little girls, and they joined her on the stage. "Our hope—our dream—is to ensure these precious little girls never need hear the words no woman can fathom. You have breast cancer."

Photographers scrambled to capture photos of the little girls, who lined up in front of Mona with hands gently clasped in front of them. Cameras flashed wildly, and the little girls smiled, and giggled.

A curtain behind Mona was raised to reveal the Diaxler Pharmaceutical Logo alongside the logo of the American Pink Ribbon Foundation, newly adorned with a tiny golden butterfly.

"Today I am pleased to announce our most promising new campaign, to date. Diaxler Pharmaceuticals, in cooperation with The American Pink Ribbon Foundation, pledge to fund a metamorphosis in breast cancer research. We aspire to transform our pink ribbons with the help of our beautiful new butterflies of hope!"

Mona raised her arm, and on cue the little girls each released a butterfly to a thunder of cheers and applause.

Seth had forced himself to sit quietly through Mona's presentation but outrage was coursing through his veins. Every muscle in his body was tense. When the little girls released their butterflies his anger got the better of him, and he started to stand up, but Amy pulled him back and held tight to his hand.

"Seth, you won't accomplish anything by making a scene. Look." she pointed to the agenda clipped to the top of the press packet. "Open house in the new research lab. Let's go see. We'll never get another chance." She narrowed her eyes at him. "That is, if you can restrain yourself."

He nodded. "I'd like to see what Mona's money can buy. It'll probably give me a case of lab-envy, though." They lost themselves in the crowd heading toward the lab.

Seth was silent while they walked across the parking

lot, not knowing how to express his utter disbelief in what he'd just witnessed. As soon as he closed the car door he started to rant.

"I'm so mad, I don't know where to begin."

Amy nodded. "I know it's sickening. But Seth, look at it this way. They're just getting started. Our research is years ahead of theirs. All we need is for one grant proposal to be funded, and you know Keri's working diligently on that. We just need one break in funding, and we'll beat them at their own game."

He turned to face her, looking intently into her eyes. "I have a question for you, and I want an honest answer."

"Of course, what is it?"

He hesitated, considering whether he should express his suspicions out loud. But this situation had been nagging at him since he'd read Mona's announcement in the newspaper.

"Do you trust Keri?"

"I do." Amy responded without hesitation. "I understand where you're coming from, and I've wondered why Mona referred her to us, but I have great intuition about people. Yes, I trust her."

"That's good to know. I think we should all have a meeting in the morning. I want to digest all I've seen, and heard today, before I talk to Bridget and Keri. But I feel it's something we should all be acutely aware of. The competition for funds just got a lot more complicated."

# CHAPTER 25

The nursing staff made Dani's hospital bed as comfortable as possible. She was dressed and waiting to go home, keeping herself busy with research on Mona's newest marketing scheme.

She clicked on a flashing, breaking news link, which took her to a video on the Denver Tribune website. It was a recording of the highlights of the press conference she'd missed just an hour earlier. *Coop must've sent Pete.*

"Humanitarian!" She said it a little too loudly, but she couldn't believe the audacity. "Holy shit! Butterflies? Are you kidding me?" Dani winced, and put her hand to her chest, "Ouch."

A nurse walking by her room stopped, and peeked in at her. "Is there something you need, Dani?"

Dani pointed to her laptop, explaining, "No, just

watching the news." She paused the video, locking it on Mona standing onstage flanked by little girls dressed head to toe in pink. *How far would you go to protect your empire, Mona Davenport?*

Charles drove them through Washington Park that afternoon, and Dani scanned every street on the way home for the gray SUV. *I'm sure the man in that car tried to hit me, or at least scare me. I have to find out who he is, and whether he's connected to the Jennings' crimes.*

Even though she didn't recognize the driver, she'd been thinking about him all morning as she struggled to piece together what she knew for certain. She felt sure these pieces were a part of the same puzzle. She just had to keep moving them around until the big picture was revealed.

She suspected the man traded in the car he used to run down Dr. Jennings at Honey's dealership. Which seemed like a good plan since no one would be looking for the gray SUV. If Honey sent that big clunker to the junkyard, the police may never find it.

Charles reached over, and stroked her hand. "Sweetheart, you seem a million miles away. Are you sure you're feeling all right? Is the car making you nervous?"

She smiled up at her husband. "I'm fine, just glad to be going home. And thank you for driving carefully over the bumps in the road. I am pretty sore."

"I know. I'm sorry. You have the rest of the week off to recover, and I can arrange to take off a few days to stay with you," he offered.

"No Charles, it's not necessary. There's really nothing you can do except hover over me, and you know I'd hate that."

The first thing Dani noticed when she walked into the living room was a beautiful bouquet of pink sweetheart roses sitting on the coffee table. She spun around to face Charles, and pointed. "Who sent those?"

"They're from Mona Davenport. She wishes you health, and a peaceful recovery. Wasn't that nice of h…"

Dani snatched the vase with a grimace, supported it with her cast, and marched to the kitchen to toss the entire arrangement into the trash. "That woman is a piece of work. I won't have any part of her, or her foundation, in my home." Her hands trembled, and her eyes brimmed with unshed tears.

Charles held her, rocking gently. "It's been a long couple of days, and you're exhausted and emotional from the trauma." He kissed her. "Let's sit down and talk about it."

She allowed him to lead her to the sofa, but she couldn't tell him she suspected her accident was orchestrated by one of Mona's puppets. She knew him well enough to know he'd watch her like a hawk, and she couldn't have him hovering while she dug into her suspicions.

"I'm sorry. I'm just emotional, probably from the drugs. And, I couldn't sleep well without you beside me." His handsome face, so full of love and concern, made her heart melt. She felt guilty about hiding things from him. *It's for your own good, Charles. The less you know, the better.*

# CHAPTER 26

Mona could hear the phones ringing before she opened the door to her offices. The receptionist rattled off a constant stream of, "American Pink Ribbon Foundation, can you hold please?" Mona smiled at her, nodded, and continued toward her office.

Jackie was on the phone, and glanced up at Mona with wide eyes and mouthed 'WOW' as she confirmed another appointment with a local TV news reporter.

Mona opened the morning newspaper on her desk, and read every word, running a finger over her broche. When she finished the well-crafted article she nodded her approval. *Nicely done, Pete. I still can't decide which is better, money or influence.* She inhaled deliciously, daydreaming of the flocks that would turn up at future events in support of her newest brainchild. *Both. This is genius.*

Jackie came in beaming, carrying two cups of coffee. "You're booked solid for two weeks. The phones haven't stopped ringing."

"Wonderful! These one-on-one interviews will be much more personal, and should ultimately get us more publicity for our newest project." She could still hear the phones ringing, "Shall we call in one of the volunteers to help with the phones?"

"Yes, maybe for a week or two," Jackie said.

"Arrange a volunteer, dear." Pushing the newspaper across the desk, Mona continued, "And have this article framed for the conference room, please."

Mona leaned back, and folded her hands on her desk. "Jackie, this is a big day for our foundation. You'll be busy. We will all be busy. Your annual review is coming up next month, but I'd like to do it now." Mona smiled warmly at the assistant who she knew would do anything for her. "Your loyalty and discretion mean everything to me, and to the work we do here. You've not had a substantial salary increase since you started at the foundation, and I'm giving you one now. Twenty-five percent, effective immediately."

Jackie jumped up off her chair and squealed, rushing around the desk to give Mona a hug. "Thank you, Mona. I don't know what to say except I'm so grateful. And you know I love working here." Her voice was shaky, and she quickly brushed a tear from her cheek.

"Yes, I know, dear. Now touch base with Keri this morning. Make sure she has the new submittal guidelines, and inquire whether the information I requested is on the way."

"I will." Jackie started toward her own desk, "And thank you for your generosity. You won't be sorry."

"Yes, I know, dear. You're welcome."

Mona slowly spun her chair around and stood up to look at the city she had captivated. It was a brilliant move, and she'd played it as strategically as a Grandmaster plays a game of Chess. She called Hastings to schedule a lunch meeting, then called the tailor to bring over fabric selections. She'd need an updated wardrobe when she talked to the world about her plans.


Mona was escorted to her table at The Capital Grille, where Todd Hastings was waiting. An open bottle of champagne was poured as soon as she was seated. "My dear, I can't remember ever having so many phone calls. Our little announcement has exceeded even my expectations." She raised her glass, "We will triumph."

"To our triumph." Todd's smile looked a little off to her, but she brushed it off as the stress of coordinating yesterday's big event.

"The attorneys are working out the precise wording to trademark. My marketing department has some brilliant ideas for the new campaign, and the phones haven't been this busy in years." Mona said.

"This has "knockout punch" written all over it." Todd said.

"Do encourage the new team to have something press-worthy ready at the end of the month. You know we need to release information regularly to stay in the news."

She smacked her hand on the table. "Oh, this is perfect timing. We can time the next press release about a week before Thanksgiving. We'll announce how thankful we are to have been able to put together such a brilliant team of researchers dedicated to eradicating this disease. Thanks to our generous supporters, of course."

He shook his head. "You are a master at what you do, Mona. I'll give you that. I am constantly surprised at the ease with which you execute."

Mona leaned in, and whispered, "Who wants to be a multi-millionaire?"

She saw the glint in his eyes. Todd was the perfect liaison since, like her, he craved power, and recognition. She knew he earned a good living as VP of Sales for Diaxler Pharmaceuticals, but he was far more ambitious. The trick was to know how to handle success, and Todd knew perfectly how to work the media without seeming ostentatious. He also knew how to rev up his sales teams, by pulling out all the stops. They understood each other very well.

She was happily relaxed after they emptied the bottle

of champagne, and he gave the waiter his credit card, then handed her his business card.

"Todd dear, I have dozens of these, what…"

"Turn it over. Look at that website when you get back to the office. Listen carefully, that site is anonymous, but the information could only have come from one source since no one else was privy to the information when this post was written. On that date, your press release had only gone out the Trib. The writing style is unmistakable."

She could see the muscles in his jaw working. "Unless someone in your organization leaked the new release early."

"My organization is loyal." Her voice quivered just the slightest bit when she demanded, "What is Hope, Incorporated?"

# CHAPTER 27

Seth couldn't help but notice Keri seemed nervous as he recounted the activities of yesterday's press conference.

"I saw part of it on the news last night," Bridget said. "And I read some of the blogs afterwards. She has a lot of support. Are you sure this means she won't also fund our project, Seth? We're ready for clinical trials, and they're just getting started. Funding us would give her a huge start on her new goal."

Keeping an eye on Keri, Seth responded, "No, Bridget. I don't think there's a chance in hell she'll fund us now. And you should see the lab she's funded for Diaxler. It's an enormous space outfitted with top of the line equipment. I have lab-envy."

"Me, too." Amy slid to the edge of her seat. "I didn't think to look at the Internet last night. Did anyone look at the blog that writes about us?"

"There's a blog about us?" Seth raised his eyebrows at the news.

Keri jumped in, "Yes, there is a blog about us, and I looked at it last night, and again this morning, but there've been no new posts for a couple of days now." Her foot tapped under the chair.

Bridget pulled a scrunchie out of her pocket, and tied up her thick mop of hair. "I wonder if the blogger will focus on the Diaxler lab now that Mona has announced she's behind prevention. It's already obvious who will get the publicity."

Keri let out a long breath, and looked down at her lap, biting her lip. "I think it's time I told you all something."

Seth's attention riveted on Keri. "We're listening." He tried to disguise the sharp tone; he knew it sounded accusatory, but his stomach was starting to churn. In spite of Amy's trust of Keri, he still wasn't sure.

Keri swallowed hard, and looked at Seth. "Mona very much wanted me to have this grant writing position. She requested a meeting with me, and I drove down from Fort Collins hoping she'd have a job for me at her foundation. I have to admit, I've wanted to work in her organization for years."

Bridget slowly removed her glasses, and looked from Seth to Keri. "Why would she care where you work?"

Keri shrugged, and shook her head slowly. "The

meeting was so strange, you guys. She made it sound like the logical thing for me to do." Her voice was shaky, and Seth was afraid she'd stop right there.

Amy reached over and rubbed Keri's shoulder. "It's all right, Keri. You're among friends here. Tell us what happened."

She looked at each of them in turn before starting again. "I can't be sure of anything of course, but Mona said she felt sorry for Bridget because she'd been passed over for the promotion given to Seth. She said she wanted to help."

Bridget looked embarrassed. "I guess I was a little disappointed for a day or two, and that's when Mona called me for lunch. Remember, Seth?"

He nodded. "I know. We've worked together for such a long time I could tell you were upset when the board promoted me. I was as surprised as anyone. I never realized the board was considering such a move."

"Yes, I know that now. Keri, I'm sorry I interrupted. Please continue."

"I never really understood, never put it together until last night when I saw the news." Keri seemed to be searching for words. "Let me back up a bit. After my first day here I knew this was the right place for me. You all made me feel so welcome, and I have to say," Keri smiled at Bridget, "even though I tried, I couldn't pick up a drop of animosity between the three of you."

Anyway," she continued, "The day I started this job Mona called me at home, and encouraged me to send her another grant proposal. I was thrilled to hear she had such an interest in the research. I told her how great you all are, how impressive the research is, and she sounded delighted to hear it. But..." Keri took in another deep breath and looked directly at Seth. "She asked me to send her the research documentation in its entirety. She said it would expedite the process when she received the new proposal."

Seth leapt from his chair, clenching his fists. "Oh, my God! YOU DIDN'T!" He shouted, and paced around the room. "Tell me you didn't do that to us, Keri! This could ruin all of us! What will I tell the Board?"

Amy flashed Seth a warning look, and turned to Keri, speaking gently. "Keri? Did you send Mona the research?"

"No!" She was emphatic. "That's what I wanted to tell you. I told her I'd have to ask Seth first." Keri stood up to face him. "And she told me not to bother you with it because you were busy. I promise you, I've been writing grants since college, and I know the protocol."

"Keri, you never discussed any of this with me. I'd remember something like that." Seth was still pacing around the office, shaking his head.

"No, I didn't mention it because you really were busy, and I knew the answer, anyway. I just ignored her request, though I expect she'll remind me about it soon. Seth, I haven't sent as much as a memo to Mona since I started my job here with you. And I promise, I won't. But considering her recent announcement I felt it was important that you know how I came to work here."

He sat down and looked at Keri apologetically, "I'm sorry I got angry. I shouldn't have shouted. Nolan would never have done that."

Bridget said, "You're not Nolan, Seth. And your reaction is completely understandable under the circumstances. It sounds like Mona intends to either steal our research, or sabotage any chance we have of getting it funded for clinical trials."

"I'm wondering if I should advise the board of directors about this." Seth was still reeling from the press conference, and now Keri's news made him question whether this research would ever see the light of day.

Keri looked panicked, but didn't say a word.

"I don't see any reason to involve the board at this point. We're all aware of the situation now," Bridget reasoned.

"I agree with Bridget." Amy said. "We all know where we stand with Mona, and her foundation. Let's just get busy, and beat her at her own game."

# CHAPTER 28

"Sleep well?" Charles sat on the edge of the bed, and set a cup of coffee on the nightstand.

"I did. It feels so good to be back in my own bed. I'm not cut out to be a patient." She noticed he was dressed for the office.

"I slept better too, knowing you were safe beside me. Are you sure you don't want me to stay home with you today?"

"I'm sure. I need to get up, move around, and work out the soreness. I can't just lie around here all day, and have you waiting on me. I think I'll be fine to go to work by tomorrow."

"Tomorrow?" He shook his head and smiled at her. "I think it might be better if you stay here, and give your body and your mind a chance to recover. Why don't you take advantage of the week Coop gave you, and do some research on a vacation for us? Maybe plan a trip around the holidays. We could spend Christmas somewhere warm, and tropical. Wouldn't that be more fun than rushing back to work?"

"Yes, but I was looking forward to covering the fire department's training burn at the old bowling alley tomorrow. I haven't covered one before, and I don't want to miss it."

"Are you sure Coop hasn't assigned that to someone else by now?" Charles looked skeptical.

"I'll call him today, and tell him I plan to be there. I can meet James on site and see how I feel afterwards. If I'm feeling lousy I'll come home, and write my piece from here."

"That sounds reasonable. We should plan a trip sometime soon, though. Think about where you might like to go." He stood up and straightened his tie. "Anything I can get you before I leave?"

"I don't think so. Oh! Yes there is. I'll need a car since the insurance company considers mine a total loss. Can you get someone at the bank to work up a loan for me? I think I'll call Honey and see what she has on the lot."

"Sounds reasonable. But please take it easy, and call me if you need anything."

Snipes eased away from the curb near the Driscoll home, keeping a safe distance from the taxicab that picked her up. *Let's see what you're up to today, Missy.*

When the cab dropped her off at Romano Chevrolet, about four yards from his old ride, his palms started to sweat. *What?* He couldn't very well drive in right behind her, so he drove around the block to gather his thoughts, finally deciding to park at the sandwich shop across the street.

As soon as he got out of his car he could see she was browsing the lot, obviously in search of a new car. *Whew! That makes sense; hers is prob'ly a wreck. Ha ha ha.*

Zach, the salesman who'd stepped in for that sweet little Honey, stuck a temporary tag on a brand new, red SUV. *Test drive. They'll be back.*

Snipes went inside to grab a sandwich, and cup of coffee, and sat on the outdoor bench in front of the building. He resisted the urge to walk across the street, and rub his hand over the well-loved Caddy. It was just sitting there now, obviously unwanted.

Moments later he choked on steaming hot coffee when the SUV returned to the lot and the reporter handed Zach a business card, then walked around the building and started taking photos of his old Caddy with her cell phone.

Watching helplessly, he sat frozen right there in front of the sandwich shop. His throat still burned from the hot coffee, and the front of his shirt was sopping wet from the spill. Snipes knew in his gut he was busted. He had to get out of Denver. *I have to get that phone first.*

Jackie was tidying up the conference room when Dani walked into the headquarters of The American Pink Ribbon Foundation, unannounced. "Good morning, Jackie. Is Mona in? I'd like to thank her for the flowers."

Jackie peeked around the corner, "Not yet, she's at a luncheon but she'll be back anytime now. How are you, Ms. Driscoll? I heard about your car accident, and it looks like you broke your arm. Can I get you anything? Coffee? Water?"

"No, thank you Jackie, I'm fine. I suppose you actually sent the flowers on Mona's behalf. They were beautiful." Her chest and ribs were aching badly, and she knew she was pushing herself after car shopping, but she wanted to confront Mona in person, and compare her reactions with her words. "Mind if I sit down while I wait?"

"Of course not. We've been so busy here since your original story on our vaccine, and of course yesterday was the big press conference. Were you there?"

"No, sadly, I missed it. I didn't get out of the hospital until after noon."

"Dani, dear!" The ever-present lilt was unmistakable, and hearing it caused a sudden wave of nerves in the pit of Dani's stomach.

"Hello Mona." Dani tried not to wince as she stood up. "Do you have a few minutes?"

"Of course, dear! Do come in." Mona shoved her coat and scarf at Jackie, and led Dani to her office. "How are you? I

216

heard about your nasty accident. It must have been awful for you."

"It was frightening, but it could have been much worse. There were children on the sidewalk. I barely missed hitting them." Dani watched Mona for any hint of remorse.

"Oh, dear! I'm glad the children are okay. I'm sure you gave them a fright." Mona glanced at her watch. "To what do I owe the pleasure?"

Dani flipped open her notepad, steeling herself for confrontation. "First, I want to thank you for sending the flowers. My husband had them sitting on the coffee table when he brought me home yesterday. Your arrangement was the first thing I saw."

Mona tilted her head sympathetically. "Of course dear, I wanted you to know I was thinking about you."

"I suppose you know I missed the press conference you held at Diaxler Pharmaceuticals, and I wanted to ask you a few questions of my own."

Mona pressed the intercom button on her phone. "Jackie, please bring Dani a press packet." She leaned back in her chair. "The press packet includes all the marvelous details, but if you have a few specific questions I do have a few minutes before I leave for New York."

"I do, actually. You've been known as one of the leaders in the quest to find a cure for breast cancer for many years." Dani carefully phrased her question. "I'm wondering why you chose not to fund the Rush vaccine, but instead decided to get behind a project that's basically starting over."

Mona toyed with her broach and didn't miss a beat. "Dear, we have a policy of not discussing grant proposals we've elected not to fund. We certainly don't want to infer anything detrimental to the Rush research but I will tell you, since I know you're one of our biggest supporters in the press. At the time of their submittal it simply did not fit our criteria. Of course, soon after we reviewed the proposal poor Dr. Jennings passed away, which made the request for funding obsolete since the primary investigator was unable to carry on."

"A convenient fact, I'm sure." Dani watched every expression, searching for telling body language, but Mona was obviously practiced at keeping her cool. "Is it simply semantics? Cure versus prevention? What exactly is your criterion for funding a project? Lucrative drugs? Awareness promotions that involve thousands of followers cheering you on with a fistful of dollars—is that your criterion?"

"My dear! What do you mean?" Mona put her hand over her chest, covering her cherished broach. "I was truly saddened by the death of Dr. Jennings. I met Bridget Mallory personally to tell her so. And as for the projects we fund..."

"I'm wondering if you know how many women will suffer, and die of breast cancer while the world waits for your new research project to catch up with the Rush vaccine, and produce a viable alternative."

Mona said nothing. She sat behind her desk, fingering her broach, looking perplexed.

"You don't know?" Dani flipped open her notepad, leaning it on the sling that supported the cast, all the while examining Mona's expressions and body language. "That's okay, I did some calculations for you. In the ten years you've estimated it will take to develop a new vaccine, three hundred ninety five thousand women will very likely die of this disease. And nearly three million more will be diagnosed with breast cancer."

Dani could feel the anger bubbling in her stomach. Her hands shook. "Oh sure, they'll be given drugs. The cures you've been funding all these years, which will drain their bank accounts, deplete their energy, and ruin their immune systems. These poor women will be treated with chemicals that take them to the brink of death. They will endure daily treatments of high-dose radiation, and have their breasts surgically removed while we wait another ten years on your newest project, which you've ironically branded with a butterfly. I want to know why." Dani demanded.

Mona's beautifully made up face went white as a sheet. "Oh dear, I believe you're suffering from the effects of your accident. Surely you don't think..."

Dani continued. "Isn't it true that the new grant writer at Rush is related to Jackie? Aren't you even a little bit concerned that might be viewed as a conflict of interest, considering you are now funding a competitor?"

"I beg your pardon." Color rushed to Mona's cheeks. "I'm afraid I must call Coop and tell him that his reporter is in my office making highly inappropriate insinuations." She reached for the phone, but Dani raised a finger.

"I'm not here on assignment for the Trib. In fact Coop has no idea I'm here. I came because I personally want answers to questions that have been haunting me for weeks. And the latest question on my mind is whether there is a reason why you didn't want me to attend your press conference, even though I received an invitation?"

Jackie hurried in, handed Dani the press packet, and turned to her boss with an expression of alarm. "Is there anything else, Mona?"

"Yes, please show Ms. Driscoll to the door. Our time is up. I must get to the airport." Mona stood, straightened her jacket, and motioned toward the door.

"Just one more thing. What do you know about this, Mona?" Dani shoved her cell phone in Mona's face, showing her the photo of the De Ville.

Mona shook her head, and raised a brow. "I think you've suffered a bigger bump on the head than you realize, dear. Now, I must be going."

Jackie reached down to take Dani gently by the arm. "This way Ms. Driscoll."

She stood up slowly, trying desperately not to reveal the pain she was feeling. She started out the door with Jackie, and turned once more toward Mona. "Have you seen the blog on the Internet called Hope Incorporated? Do you know who the blogger is?"

She had just a moment to take one last look at Mona before Jackie took a firmer grip on her arm. Her knowing glare was stone cold.

*Gotcha!*

Keeping a close eye on the reporter, Snipes fished a clean t-shirt out of the duffle bag in the back seat, and pulled it over his head. He watched as she got out of the car, adjusted the sling on her left arm, and entered the large office building carrying only her cellphone and a notepad.

Curious, he sauntered into the lobby, studied the building directory, shrugged, and went back to his car to call his employer on the disposable cell phone. He left a message. "Need a drop tonight. Same place."

He'd saved a bundle, spending only what he absolutely needed to get by, and now he had plenty of cash stashed to make the trip north. *Pays good, but getting too risky. Lake Louise, here I come.*

Snipes sneered as she limped back to her car. *In a little pain, are you, girlie?*

He watched her ease herself down on the side of the

seat and rub her knee for a moment. Finally, she closed the door, buckled up, and drove out of the parking lot.

Snipes devised a plan to grab the evidence that connected him to the hit and run, as he followed her toward Washington Park.

He parked around the block when she reached her home, and crept around the north side of the house, hopefully obscured by the tall evergreens. *Bingo*! Peering out between the branches, he saw her sitting alone on the porch, holding that damned phone. *Whose idea was it to put cameras in phones anyway? No privacy anywhere.*


Dani pulled her new SUV into the driveway, and sat for a moment behind the steering wheel, trying to muster the energy to move. She sent Terrell a text. "I need to show you something."

She slowly made her way to the front porch. The chill air felt good on her sore body. Easing herself into the porch swing, she checked her cell phone for email while she waited for a text from Terrell.

Five minutes later Terrell pulled his unmarked car in front of the house. "Dani-girl!" He pointed to the SUV. "That your new ride?" He nodded his approval. "Nice. Red suits you."

*Damn! I wasn't expecting him to stop by with his partner.*

"Do you know my partner, Regina Collins? We're on the clock, but since we were already in the area, I thought I'd just drop by." They each took a porch chair opposite Dani. "What'd you want to show me? Your new car?"

Dani smiled. "We've never met. It's a pleasure to meet you, Regina."

She had hoped to keep this between friends, but found the photo and handed him her cell phone. "Is this the car from the hit and run?"

He let out a long whistle. "Sure looks like it, but I'd have to compare this with the pics from the file. What do you think, Collins?" He handed her Dani's phone.

"Color, make, and model look right to me. And it's banged up like the one from the surveillance camera." She handed the phone back to Dani. "Terrell's right, we'll have to do a side by side comparison of the photos to be sure."

Terrell stood up. "Email that to me, will you? Where on God's green earth did you find this?"

"I'm a reporter; I followed the clues. Besides, I have great intuition. No offense, but it's a girl thing." She grinned at Collins and sent the email. "There you go. Sent."

He chuckled and shook his head. "No offense taken. Good detective work. Hey, let me see that again." He flipped through the photos on Dani's phone. "I recognize this place in the background. It's..." Terrell turned when he heard Charles drive up. "Romano Chevrolet?"

Dani nodded. "Uh huh. On the used car side."

"There's an unmarked police car parked in front of my house. What's my wife done now?" Charles bent down and kissed her.

Dani gave Terrell a warning look. "You know me, I can never manage to stay out of mischief. Charles, this is Detective Regina Collins. They were just in the neighborhood."

"We need to get back to the station, and wrap up." Terrell started toward the porch steps. "You two take care now."

Charles eased himself down beside her, and nodded toward the new car. "Looks like you've had a productive day. Bright red. I like it. I sent Honey the funds this afternoon. How are you feeling?"

"Pretty sore. Tired. But otherwise I'm fine. Want to take it for a spin? Maybe pick up Chinese for dinner?" She batted her eyelashes, and tucked her cellphone into her jacket pocket.

Snipes worked his way between the trees. Just as he stepped toward the side yard, a big sedan pulled up right in front of the house. He jerked back behind his cover, and peered out between the prickly needles. *An unmarked police car. Shit!*

He had to steady himself by holding onto a dead tree limb, and it snapped, nearly dumping him in the yard before he caught his balance. Easing backward into the trees, he turned too quickly and a pine needle jabbed him in the eye. *Dammit to hell!*

The sting of it made his eye water profusely, and he wiped it with the sleeve of his t-shirt. He held his breath, peering between the branches as two detectives walked toward the porch. *Calm down.* Snipes slowly expelled his breath, relieved that they hadn't noticed him.

The relief was short lived. He stood helplessly behind his prickly cover, his chest filling with dread, when he saw her hand the cell phone over to one of the detectives. The phone passed back and forth between the three of them while they pointed, and discussed whatever had brought them there.

After about ten minutes, the detectives handed the cell phone back to the reporter, and drove off.

Snipes mopped the tears from his stinging eye with his sleeve, and watched from his vantage point as the bitch and her stuffy looking husband got into the brand new car, and drove off.

Looking around to make sure no one was watching, he crept around the house and tried the back door. *Unlocked. Score!* Pumping his fist in victory he took off his shoes, careful not to leave tracks, and let himself into the kitchen, traipsing around the house silently in his socks, observing.

He rummaged around in desk drawers until he found her business card with several phone numbers listed. He tucked the card in his shirt pocket. *I'll call her and lure her outside later. I won't have any trouble snatching the phone from her in her condition.*

Noting the layout of the house, he surveyed the place for a souvenir.

Slinking up the staircase, he reached the open loft and poked his head through the doorways of two spare bedrooms. He slipped into the master suite, and opened the walk-in closet. *WTF! How many shoes does one bitch need?* He ran his hand over the long row of starched, and neatly pressed men's dress-shirts, and stopped to slip on a flannel-lined denim jacket, nodding in approval. *Fits good. Perfect for the trip.*

Snipes heard a car slow down outside. He leapt to the window, peeking between the large white shutters in time to see The Suit walking around the SUV to help his wife. "Shit!"

Snipes bolted down the stairs and tumbled to the floor, hitting it hard when his socks slid on the hardwood at the bottom. He could hear them talking on the other side of the door, not five feet away, and he clambered to his feet, dashing around the corner toward the kitchen, just as he heard the key turn in the front door.

"Did you hear something?" He heard the reporter ask.

Scooping up his shoes on the move, Snipes ran full out in his socks, all the way to his car.

Charles set the bag of takeout on the kitchen counter.

226

"Sweetheart, you must've left the back door open." He scanned the backyard briefly, and closed the door.

# CHAPTER 29

The four-hour flight to New York gave Mona time to gather her composure. She opened her laptop, drafted personal email to her most ardent supporters, and attached copies of her impressive talk show itinerary, which had also been posted to the website.

The latest press release had opened doors like no other project she'd devised in all her years as CEO of her foundation. She had no doubt it would net the biggest returns. Every major network wanted her on air, and some of the most respected reporters on television had requested interviews.

After checking into her suite at The Four Seasons, Mona ordered room service and gazed out at the city lights shimmering below. She'd been to New York on a number of occasions, but this time was different. This time she felt as if she belonged. This time she felt like a celebrity.

She had selected the Four Seasons because it was the tallest hotel in New York, and its reputation for opulence was unsurpassed. She dared not book the penthouse–not yet. But her view of the city from the forty-ninth floor was intoxicating.

Her meal was delicious. She finished every bite, poured a second glass of red wine, and ran a bath, sprinkling a handful of lavender bath salts in the luxurious marble tub. It was a beautiful suite, and she deserved this indulgence after spending years clawing her way among the top contenders of cancer charities. Hers was in the top ten now but she had her eye on the prize. Number one. She knew without a doubt she'd reach that coveted spot with this new campaign. *What's the point of settling for less?*

She placed the cherished broach on the marble counter and sank into the fragrant, relaxing bath. The city lights looked like a blanket of sparkling diamonds. *I think I'll make a little trip to Tiffany tomorrow afternoon. Why not? I deserve something nice after everything I've put up with all these years.*

Sipping from the fine crystal wine glass, Mona pondered the events of the last couple of months. *After tomorrow, everything will fall into place, and Dani Driscoll and her vicious little blog will be nothing more than a pesky detail.*

Gazing out over the most amazing view she'd ever seen, a sense of belonging washed over her. *I'll be able to afford to retire, and live anywhere in the world in a few short years. New York is looking better by the minute.*

"When we come back, we'll talk with the woman making new strides in the battle against breast cancer." Natalie Kramer stood up to let the crew re-arrange the set, accepted the fresh set of notes from one of the staff, and motioned Mona to sit in the chair beside her.

Mona beamed at the camera, running her fingers over her broach from time to time, and let her well-honed instincts take over. "I'm thrilled to be here, Natalie. Thank you for the warm welcome."

"Well, you've made a very exciting announcement, and we'd love to hear more about your newest campaign. Do I understand that you'll be funding research that may someday prevent breast cancer from occurring?" Natalie set her notes on the coffee table in from of them and settled back in her chair.

"That's exactly what we plan to do. This is a big step in a new direction for us. The research we've funded over the years has seen quite a lot of success, and I'm grateful to our many supporters who have made those successes possible. As you know, todays' chemotherapies offer women, and men, hope of survival. Many patients go on to live long, productive lives, due to the research we've funded. I'm very proud of my life's work."

"But you're no longer talking about a cure, are you?"

"Not at all, and that's the exciting part, isn't it? A member of my advisory board had knowledge of a scientist in Germany who is confident that a vaccine can be developed. One that can prevent breast cancer from developing."

Natalie continued. "That's remarkable. How long will it take before I can get this vaccine from my gynecologist, or primary care physician?"

"These things do take time. As you may have heard, Diaxler Labs is taking on the project, and they estimate it will take about ten years to develop the vaccine, and complete thorough laboratory testing. This is vitally important. This is a long-term project, and once we have favorable results in mice models, we plan an ongoing campaign to fund the process of FDA approval for clinical trials. Our work is hardly over—in fact this new phase is just beginning."

"So, in ten years we can be vaccinated against breast cancer at the same time we get our pap smears?"

"It's too early to predict the details of a timeline. Three phases of clinical trials will be necessary before the FDA approves it for general use. That could take another five to ten years, depending on how many women sign up for the trials."

Natalie nodded. "This is certainly an exciting development. Tell us more about your campaign. Will America be running, biking, or hiking to prevent breast cancer?"

Mona beamed. "We'll launch a wide variety of activities over the next few years so we can include everyone who wishes to participate. But, we thought we'd start off with..."

Mona reached into the basket beside her chair, and pulled out a pink polo shirt adorned with the updated logo. "Natalie, I'm pleased to present you with the official golf shirt for our first annual Tournament for Prevention. I met with our New York office early this morning, and they are prepared to sign up participants for the tournament today.

She looked directly into the camera. "And for your viewers, our staff is planning events in every major city in the country."

The staff applauded behind the cameras.

Mona smiled brightly. "I have one for each of you," she said, passing them out to the other journalists on the set.

"I feel a little healthy competition brewing among the staff already. Thank you for sharing your news with America, Mona. You have certainly proven that if anyone can pioneer a prevention for breast cancer, it's you, and your foundation."

Mona was able to carve out an afternoon of shopping, and Tiffany was her first stop. She couldn't resist the flagship store on Fifth Avenue where polished glass cases displayed the most dazzling collection of diamonds she's ever seen.

"I'd be happy to show you any piece at all, Ms. Davenport." A statuesque, and impeccably dressed saleswoman offered her assistance.

Mona smiled at the recognition. "Thank you, dear. I adore this diamond bracelet." She tapped her manicured finger on the glass.

The woman removed the bracelet and clasped it securely around Mona's wrist. "These are princess cut diamonds, flawlessly matched. It's a stunning piece."

The sales woman continued. "I want to tell you what a beautiful thing you are doing for women. I admire you more than you can imagine. I have since my aunt went through breast cancer treatment a few years ago. But now, thanks to you, I have hope that I'll never be as sick as she was."

"Oh, I'm sorry to hear that, dear. And, your aunt? Is she a survivor?"

"Yes, but her immune system is weakened now, and she gets sick more easily than she did before. Our family is thankful she's still with us, and we all participated in your New York event last year. We plan to do it every year until we no longer have to."

"Thank you, dear. Your support means a lot to me, and even more to the women who are diagnosed each year."

"How does the bracelet feel? It looks lovely on you."

Mona held her arm out to admire the brilliant diamonds. "Thank you, dear. It is a beautiful piece. Can you show me some earrings? Nothing overly elaborate; maybe some princess cut solitaires to go with the bracelet."

Mona walked out of Tiffany wearing a $16,000

bracelet, a $5,500 pair of coordinating diamond earrings, feeling like a million bucks.

# CHAPTER 30

Terrell and Collins drove around the lot at Romano Chevrolet on the way back to the station.

"I don't see it anywhere," Collins said. "Let me see that email."

Terrell pulled along side of the building thumbing through the email on his cell phone. "Here are the photos Dani sent. It's probably gone already. Dealerships like Romano's don't like to keep junkers on their lots very long. Let's go inside–see if the salesman's here."

All eyes were on the two detectives as they entered the showroom. The manager promptly came out to greet them, and Collins flashed her badge.

"Is there something I can help you with, detectives?"

"We're looking for the salesperson who took this in on trade." Terrell held out his phone, displaying one of the photos of the DeVille.

He nodded, "Sure. Let's take this conversation to my office." As they passed the receptionist he told her to find Zach.

"Please have a seat. Can I get you anything? Water? Coffee? There may be some donuts left in the service department."

Collins rolled her eyes at her partner with a slight shake of her head. "No, we just have a few questions about the person who traded in that vehicle."

Zach leaned in the doorway, wide eyed. "You asked for me?"

"Yes Zach, these police detectives have some questions about the guy who traded in the old DeVille."

"Where's the vehicle now?" Terrell started the questioning.

"These cars are useless for re-sale. We delivered it to the junkyard late this afternoon." The manager consulted his computer, wrote the name and address of the junkyard on the back of his business card, and handed it to Terrell.

"Who traded it in, and what vehicle did the guy leave here with?" Collins jotted on a small notepad she drew from her shirt pocket.

"I remember him," Zach started. "He only took one car for a test drive and he bought it on the spot. A two-year old gray Escape. Easiest sale I ever made. The guy paid cash, had a huge roll of money on him. I've never seen anyone carry around that much cash before."

Collins nodded. "Do you have a name for us? Do you remember it, Zach?"

Zach looked skyward, like he was trying to pull the information out of memory. "Al, Al... it was something unusual but he went by his last name. Snipes, I think."

Terrell looked at the manager. "We'll need the VIN on that Escape. Actually, a copy of the registrations on both vehicles, and a copy of his drivers license should have everything we need."

The manager looked skeptical. "I take it this is part of an ongoing investigation?"

Terrell was honest. "It is, and I understand your position. I can get a warrant if you prefer."

"No. That won't be necessary. I'm happy to help. I'll have the secretary make copies for you."

Collins turned her attention to the young salesman, still leaning in the doorway, obviously feeling very important. "Is there anything else you can tell us, Zach? Anything he might have mentioned when you went on the test drive with him?"

"He didn't talk much. Most customers make small talk during a test drive, or they ask questions about the car. I do remember him saying he was moving back to the mountains, though. That's why he wanted a four-wheel drive."

"Did he say where?" Collins continued to make notes.

"Not really. But, he did say a road trip would be involved." Zach was rocking from one foot to the other now.

Terrell looked at Collins with a knowing glance. *Time is of the essence.*

They stood up and Collins took the copies from the receptionist. She thumbed through to the copy of the driver's license, and showed it to Zach. "Is this the guy who traded in the DeVille?"

"Yeah, that's him. I think he's been working out since that photo though. He's not huge but he seemed plenty strong. "Hey, what'd this guy do, anyway?"

Terrell ignored the question. "Zach, here's my card. Call me immediately if you think of anything else about this man. You've been very helpful."

They climbed back into the cruiser, and Terrell blew out a long breath. "You up for a long night?"

"Nothing waiting for me at home except re-runs, and bottle of beer. Let's do it." Collins reached for her communications radio.

She called dispatch and arranged for a forensics team meet them at the junkyard to dust for prints, and anything else they could find. Then she ran the drivers license through the system.

"We have an ex-con on our hands. An ex-con carrying around a roll of cash. The way I add this up, we could be smack in the middle of a homicide investigation. The hit and run that resulted in the death of Dr. Jennings might not have been an accident. I'm thinking murder for hire."

"What's on his rap sheet?" Terrell kept his eyes on the road, but he was thinking about his conversation with Dani.

"Attempted robbery. Served two years—got out less than a year ago. That's it."

"Attempted robbery to homicide? It's a stretch but I don't like this, Collins. I don't like it one bit. Dani's up to her eyeballs digging into this thing. She thinks there's a conspiracy around the research Jennings was doing. I just thought she was on one of her soapboxes again. You know, like saving the planet from pollution—something along those lines. I don't even want to think about what could happen if... Call in and ask about the vehicle that almost ran her over, will you?"

When they arrived at the junkyard, an attendant was just locking the gate on the chain link fence. They flashed their badges, and asked about the DeVille.

The young attendant leaned against the gate and pointed in the direction of the vehicle he'd taken in earlier. "We open at 7:30 in the mornin'."

Terrell shook his head. "I'm afraid this can't wait 'til morning. Call the boss and let him know we're here. Maybe he'll come in and let you go home."

"Boss is outta town." His look was pleading. Like he'd been sitting in the trailer-office all day, bored out of his mind, and was ready for an evening of socializing with friends.

"I understand. What's your name?" Collins asked.

"Johnnie."

"Well Johnnie, you wouldn't want your boss to return and ask you why the police had to ram the gate to gain access, would you?" Collins made her point.

"You would do that?" Johnnie asked.

Collins raised her eyebrows.

"Okay, come on in." He unlocked the gate and looked up at the forensics van pulling in. "Is this gonna take long?"

"It will take as long at it takes." Terrell said.

The comm radio sounded, "Collins?"

"Collins. Go ahead."

"That would be a gray Ford Escape. Witnesses put it at two to three years old."

"Copy that."

Fear turned over in Terrell's gut.

# CHAPTER 31

The sound of a vibration coming from her nightstand woke Dani up. *Who would call at this hour?*

Scowling, she slipped out of bed, snatched her cell phone, and tiptoed to the hallway.

"Hello?" Noting the time on her phone. *Almost two a.m.*

"Who is this?" A man's voice responded on the other end.

In an irritated whisper she replied, "You called me and it's the middle of the night. Who is this?"

"Now listen carefully. I have some important information for the reporter. Is this the reporter?"

Dani crept down the stairs, not wanting to wake Charles. "Yes, I work for the Tribune. What do you want? And why are you calling my cell phone at this hour instead of calling my office during business hours?"

She turned on the light in her study and eased herself down at her desk with the phone wedged between her ear, and shoulder. She reached for a pen and paper, "Okay, I'm ready, what is it that couldn't wait 'til morning?"

"You know what it's about. But I can't tell you on the phone. Check your front porch for an envelope."

*Knows who I am.* The thought was fleeting, dissipating before she could grasp it.

Dani rolled her eyes, and stood up slowly. Her shoulder ached without the sling to support the weight of the cast on her arm.

She flipped the switch to the porch light, but it didn't turn on. "Damn," she whispered. *Forgot to change that light bulb.*

She craned her neck to peer out the peephole. "No, there's nothing on my front porch. Look, why don't you call my office tomorrow and..."

"On the swing." The voice on the other end sounded as irritated as she was feeling right about now.

The wind sent autumn leaves scurrying across the porch when Dani stepped into the cool night air. She shivered, wishing she'd pulled her robe over her pajamas. Clouds moved across the moon and the only light was a distant streetlamp, making it difficult to see in the shadows of the covered porch.

Walking barefoot to the porch swing, she scanned the

area and looked under the swing. "No, you must have the wrong house. Or the wrong reporter. I'm hanging up now."

Shivering, she turned to go back inside, but a faint noise in the corner behind the swing caught her attention. *Probably the neighbor's cat.*

"Blackie?" She leaned to one side to investigate, and dropped her cell phone when two gloved hands shot out of the darkness, grabbed her by the shoulder and clamped over her mouth.

She bit down hard, freeing herself for an instant before he caught her by the arm, swinging her around, and slamming her into the porch swing. Pain cut through her arm and shoulder, and she struggled with the masked man, swinging with her free arm, and kicking furiously.

He yanked her from the swing by her ankles. Her head crashed hard into the swing before she landed on the concrete floor of the porch with her cast caught underneath her.

Struggling for focus, she kicked with all the strength she had, clawing at the floor, desperate to escape the stranger's firm grasp. She reached for her phone but it slid across the porch–just out of reach. She felt a warm trickle moving down her forehead, toward her eyes.

"Charles!" She shrieked, but his harsh hand muffled her cry. She instinctively bit down again, as hard as she could, tearing through the glove until she could taste blood.

"Sonofabitch!"

He jerked back his hand, and slapped her so hard across the face she felt dizzy. Fear grew in the pit of her stomach as she fought to stay alert.

He secured a heavy black scarf around her mouth, and with one swift movement flipped her over to bind her hands together tight behind her back. Pain seared through her shoulder and arm. Two fingers on her left hand went numb.

Dani frantically kicked at the porch swing, hoping to bang it against the exterior of the house and make enough noise to wake Charles. But she was dragged to her feet and shoved toward the steps before she could make contact with it.

Her head throbbed when she turned to look at him. She understood, even in the confusion, that she needed to register every detail. But, the night was too dark. Only his eyes were visible through the ski mask. *Focus! What color are his eyes?*

*So dizzy.* Her vision blurred when he spun her around and shoved her down the porch steps. Dani struggled to break free of him, but he was stronger than she, and the pain in her chest and arm took her breath away. When her knees buckled, he hefted her over his shoulder, and moved quietly toward the trees on the north side of the house.

Dani kicked at him fiercely, gasping for breath, knowing her chances of survival lessened with each step he carried her away from her home.

He dumped her into the back seat of an SUV, standing at the door long enough to bind her ankles. The familiar scent of fireplaces burning filled her nostrils. *Home. It smells like home.* Tears spilled down her cheeks while a neighbor's dog barked a furious a warning.

Her captor drove her off, into the night.


The pain in her shoulders from being tied so tightly was excruciating. Working her hands in the ropes, Dani tried to restore enough circulation to get the feeling back into them. The scarf tied around her mouth smelled faintly of men's cologne. She shivered in her pajamas, not sure whether it was because she was cold, or scared, or both.

Dani peered intently out the window of the SUV, trying to identify where she was being driven. He had ordered her to lie down in the back seat, but from her vantage point she recognized familiar businesses illuminated in the night.

When the SUV stopped at a red light, she attempted to sit up, hoping someone in another lane would look over and see her bound and gagged in the back seat.

"Stay down you snooping bitch!" His roar cut through the stillness of the night. She stifled a sob in her throat. He'd pulled the ski mask up on his head like a cap, and she blinked rapidly, trying to clear her blurred vision enough to see his face. He faced forward, so she tried to sit up again, hoping he'd turn around.

Instead he screamed, "Lay down and stay down, or I'll stop this car and knock you out with my fist."

She felt dried blood on her forehead; her head still throbbed from banging it on the porch swing.

*The swing. It's peaceful rocking back and forth, back and forth.* Dani's eyes drooped slowly. *No! Stay awake!*

*I-25. We're on the interstate.* Her eyes opened wide. Understanding snapped her brain into focus as she wondered how far he would take her. What he planned to do with her. She had always been glad it wasn't her job to cover kidnappings. The outcomes were too often brutally painful. *The woods outside the city? A secluded mountain pass?*

The nausea rolling in her stomach was vicious. A cold sweat broke over her and she felt as though she might pass out. She shivered. Her knee ached and tugged at her heart. *Mom? Dad? Can you see what's happening?*

Her heart pounded so hard she was convinced he must be able to hear it. *Charles? Are you awake?* Willing herself to ignore the sick churning in her stomach, she focused on an escape plan. *Think! Can't get to the taillights to kick them out. What else?*

Dani struggled to see her surroundings in the dark, searching for anything that might be useful. She needed to find something that could be used as a weapon, but the backseat was pristine. Not even an empty cardboard coffee cup.

*A strobe light! A siren! Someone's coming for me!*

She saw his head turn toward the rear view mirror, and the car slowed.

"Stay down!" He ordered.

The siren grew loud, louder, flashing lights replaced darkness, but her hope dissolved, sinking to the bottom of her churning stomach, when her captor exited the interstate as the ambulance passed them at full speed.

Fear pulsed through every cell of her body. Panic overtook reasonable thought when she realized they had slowed, and were driving over broken pavement. Dani choked back tears, straining to see anything identifiable outside the window, but it was too dark and she was still lying in the backseat.

The car slowed to a stop. Her abductor opened his door, got out, then slammed it shut.

Dani pushed herself up, watching him walk around the car and open her passenger door. *Charles! Help me! Are you awake? Are you looking for me? Somebody please help me!*

# CHAPTER 32

Charles woke with a jerk to the sound of the doorbell followed by someone pounding on the door. "What the...?"

He trotted down the stairs, pulling a robe over his boxers, calling out, "I'm coming, I'm coming!" When he yanked open the door to find Terrell standing in front of him, he was confused.

"Terrell? Come in, what's wrong?"

Terrell looked as if he'd pulled an all-nighter. "I need to speak with both of you. I know your wife is tired and sore, but I need her down here now."

"What's this about? Did you find out something about her accident?" Charles tied his robe and headed toward the kitchen. "I need coffee, and you look like you need a triple espresso."

"Dani needs to hear this, too. I'll put on some coffee

while you get her up."

"Dani?" Charles checked the master bedroom and bath, but his wife wasn't there. A chill ran through him as he ran back down the stairs to her study. Her computer and satchel were sitting where she'd left them last night. All at once the silence of the early morning hour became deafening. His breath came fast but was so shallow only a whisper came out. "Sweetheart?"

He found Terrell in the kitchen getting cups out of the cabinet. "She must be out back if you didn't see her on the porch."

Terrell threw open the back door. "She's not upstairs?"

"No. Maybe she left a note on the fridge. She wanted to cover the fire department's practice burn this morning, but six a.m. is an early start, even for her." Charles tried to calm himself; tried to reason things out before he had to admit to himself what his heart already knew.

"Her car's still parked out front, Charles. Let's check the house, one room at a time." Terrell said. "You check upstairs and I'll check the basement."

Charles heard him calling out, "Dani-girl!"

Charles raced up the stairs two at a time, hoping he'd missed seeing her in the shower in his confusion. "Dani, are you okay? Where are you, Sweetheart?"

By the time he reached the kitchen again his hands were trembling. "Her computer is here, her purse and satchel are in her study." Then he remembered. Terrell had come to tell them something. "Where is she, Terrell? What's going on?"

"Sit down, Charles. I'm gonna call this in. When was the last time you saw her?"

"I think we finally got to sleep around eleven last night. We were exhausted from the past few days, and I took an over the counter sleeping pill. But, I can't believe that I slept so hard I didn't hear her get out of bed." He felt the blood draining from his face, and he shook his head, trying to deny what he already knew at his core. "How could I have slept through my wife getting up and leaving the house?"

Terrell put a hand on his friend's shoulder. "She's not officially considered missing until eleven o'clock tonight. But, I consider her missing, and if I have to take the day off to find her, that's what I'll do."

The panic that had been simmering inside suddenly exploded in fear. "Terrell, stop! Tell me what's going on right now. What's happened to my wife?"

Terrell motioned him to sit down at the kitchen table. "Okay, Charles. This is a lot to take in. The pieces of our investigation are coming together, and it's very possible Dani was right about a conspiracy to keep the Jennings research out of the press. There is enough evidence now for me to believe someone may have tried to put a lid on his research. We're looking at the Jennings accident as a possible homicide."

His mouth gapped; he was speechless. But, in spite of his external silence, warring thoughts clashed so painfully in his head he felt dizzy. He managed a whisper, "Where is she?"

"I'm sorry to say I don't know. But we'll find her, Charles. We'll find her."

# CHAPTER 33

When her captor opened the door to pull her out of the vehicle, he'd already disguised his face with the ski mask again. Dani searched for something distinguishable about him, but he was dressed head to toe in black, and making out details in the dark was impossible.

She kicked at him with bound feet when he leaned in to grab her. It was enough to make him take a step back.

He spoke to her sternly. "Now, listen carefully. You will cooperate; you have no choice. This is what we're going to do. I will untie your ankles and you will walk, not run, do you hear me? We'll walk inside together. Do you understand?"

*Inside?* She craned her neck to look past him, squinting to make out any detail that might clue her in on where he'd driven her. She nodded, fully intending to flee.

Her body hurt so bad every movement was painful.

She watched the holes in the mask for a glimpse of his identity, and slowly straightened her legs to allow him to unbind her feet.

Once her legs were free he reached in for her shoulders, and she knew if she was going to escape, this might be her only chance. Dani snapped her legs to her chest then thrust her feet hard into his stomach, knocking him backward to the ground.

Scrambling out of the back of the SUV she quickly assessed her surroundings. Warm relief spread though her when she saw the old abandoned bowling alley, knowing that in a matter of hours this place would be swarming with firemen, reporters, and members of the Chamber of Commerce. *And Charles. Charles please find me.*

*Run! Don't look back. Find a place to hide.*

She ran flat out toward the building, ignoring the pain of loose gravel on her bare feet, praying the door would be unlocked, and she could secure herself inside. The double glass doors were in sight now.

Excruciating pain shot through her knee. She limped a few steps, then sprinted through the pain, to reached the doors. Struggling to reach the door-pull with her arms tied behind her, her heart sank. It was too high; she couldn't reach it.

"You bitch!" His scream pierced the night. "That's not what I said! You'll pay for that."

Terrified, she sank to the ground, her back against the doors. There was nowhere to go.

He seized her by the arms, hoisted her over his shoulder, and carried her inside, locking the door behind them.

Every step he took echoed in the empty darkness. Debris broke and scattered under his feet. Hanging from his shoulder all she could see was the filthy floor, abandoned bowling shoes and balls, and balled up empty snack bags.

He stopped, dropping her on the edge of a large, gritty table. Every bone in her body ached, and she shivered in her flannel pajamas.

"Do you have any idea how much trouble you've caused?" He bent over, holding his stomach, breathing hard.

She watched him, noting her surroundings, assessing her chances of getting away from him in her bound and barefoot condition. She tried to talk through the scarf and got the result she was hoping for.

"No one will hear you in here. Scream all you want." He untied the scarf and draped it over her shoulders. "Cold?"

Her mouth felt like it was full of cotton, but she managed a relieved, "Thank you."

Tentatively, making an effort to steady her voice, she asked, "Who are you? What do you want with me?"

"What do I want with you?" His words were measured; she could tell he was trying to control his temper. "Listen carefully, and I'll tell you exactly what I want." He leaned over her, within an inch of her face and screamed. "SILENCE!"

The single word shattered the eerie quiet of the abandoned building, echoing in the dark, and she cowered away from him, trembling. *Don't lose control. You have to stay calm.*

She answered his rage in a quiet voice, just above a whisper. "Silence? But, I've been bound and gagged until now. What are you talking about?" She knew if she could keep him talking long enough someone would find them.

He pulled at the ski mask, trying to fan his face. "Poking around in business that doesn't concern you; that silly little blog. What's it gonna take to convince you to let this go?"

Dizzying terror flashed through her head. *I know who you are.*

*Focus! Brown. His eyes are brown.* Dani fought through the panic and forced herself to keep a conversation going.

"You're right. It is a silly little blog. I'll take it down; just let me go. I have no idea who you are. I can't identify you. Let me walk out of here, and I promise to take down the blog."

He laughed. "You should have thought about that before. Don't worry, I'll take it down." He fished a flask from his pocket, took a long pull then offered it to her. "Want some?"

"No. I don't suppose you have any water." Her mouth

was thick with fear; she was intent on studying his body language for something recognizable.

"Sorry. No water."

Beams of light moved through the room when headlights of an occasional car drove past the bowling alley on I-25. She focused on his face, waiting for another car to drive by, and hitched a breath when his eyes were illuminated.

*There is something familiar. What is it? Think Dani, think!*

As if reading her mind he tugged her off the table. "Okay, time to get this show on the road."

She hobbled over broken glass, cutting her feet as he led her over the grimy floor. "Stop! I'm not wearing any shoes. Please slow down."

"Have it your way." He shoved her into one of the filthy conference chairs, nearly toppling it over.

She kicked at him but he pain in her arm and shoulder rendered her too weak make an impact.

He snatched the scarf from her shoulders, using it to tie her feet to the wheelbase, and then wheeled her into the utility room. She shivered when he spun her around and leaned in close. So close she could smell cologne. "Don't worry, I'll be right back."

She called after him. "Let me go! Please just let me go while it's still dark. You can leave. No one will see you in the dark!"

Frantic, she tried to wheel herself to the door, but her feet were secured to the top of the wheelbase, and as hard as she tried, she couldn't touch her toes to the floor. Working her ankles, she felt the scarf loosening, but he returned before she could free herself. He was carrying a rope.

"Miss me?"

Dani rocked violently in the chair.

"Stop squirming!"

She squeezed her eyes closed and cowered when he raised his hand to her face. She forced herself to sit still, though her heart was pounding.

He lowered his hand. "That's better."

Opening her eyes when the slap didn't come, she said, "Why are you doing this? You said yourself you were capable of shutting down my blog." She pleaded. "Why not let me go. I swear, if you let me go I'll never write another word on that blog."

She searched his eyes for any sign of sympathy, but they were stone cold.

"Why do you care about the blog, anyway?" She asked.

"Okay. That's a fair question. You want to know—I'll tell you. By tomorrow it won't matter anyway. I got a call from a friend of yours. She said you were dead set on shutting down her efforts to fund important research. Did you really mean to be "dead set"?" He curled his fingers in front of her face, making mock quotation marks in the air.

She could hear pent up anger in his voice. Horrifying understanding made her dizzy. She wasn't getting out of here; he planned to kill her. She had nothing to loose. She had to know the instincts she'd counted on her whole life had not let her down.

"So I was right all along–Mona's behind this."

He was bent over, binding her feet to the wheelbase again, this time with the rope he'd brought in from the car.

"Did Mona also hire you to run down Dr. Jennings? Did you break into the Jennings residence after he died, looking for his research? You won't get away with any of this. The police have photos of the car you used in those crimes–the one you traded in."

He stood; apparently satisfied she was secured to the chair. He seemed to take pleasure in the power he had over her.

Dani continued her interrogation. "I have to know– how much did she pay you? What's a life worth these days? Fifty thousand? A hundred-thousand? Two-fifty?"

Taking stock of her position, tied to a chair in the dark with a murderer, she whispered. "You're going to kill me, aren't you?"

His eyes were brown. But, she sensed more than that. Evil lurked behind them–she could see it, feel it. He uttered two words that should have offered relief, but filled her with terror instead. "No need."

The utility room had no windows but she could see light beginning to seep in through the windows in the adjoining room.

He wrapped the scarf around her mouth, stifling any further discussion or pleading. *Or screams.* Then he retrieved two items from his pocket. Car keys, and her cell phone. Tossing her phone on the floor, her kidnapper turned on his heel, straightened his shoulders and walked out, locking the door behind him.

# CHAPTER 34

Charles was grateful to see Terrell taking command of a full-out investigation after convincing his Commander that Dani's disappearance could be connected to the Jennings cases. Crime scene investigators combed the entire home for evidence.

Forensics had just arrived at the house and Charles listened, horrified as they talked about the aspects of several cases that Terrell now suspected were connected to Dani's disappearance.

Collins arrived, looking tired and passing out coffee. "We have an APB out on Dani Driscoll, the gray Ford Escape, and the suspect, Alistair Snipes."

*Dani where are you?*

Terrell turned to him. "Call her cell phone. We need to find it if it's here in the house. If it is we can check it for clues.

Phone calls, text messages, email, anything that might help us find her."

Charles stood up, not knowing if his shaking legs would carry him. He dashed up the stairs, grabbed his phone off the nightstand and pressed the only number in his favorites. He walked quietly from her study to the kitchen, listening for her phone to ring, and re-dialed when it went to voice mail.

"She must have her phone with her. That's good, right? She can call me." He clenched his cell phone so tight his knuckles were white.

Terrell answered, "Yes, that's good. If she has her cell phone we can track her through its signal."

Charles slumped down into a kitchen chair and dialed again, with shaking hands. "Dani pick up, pick up."

Collins put her hand over the phone, and ended the call. "If she can call, she will. We don't want to run the battery down on her phone. I know this is hard, but you have to sit tight."

He nearly dropped his phone when it rang. "Dani?"

Terrell mouthed, "Is that Dani?"

He shook his head, trying to comprehend what he was hearing. "Can you repeat that?" He shoved the phone into Terrell's outstretched hand.

Terrell nodded, hung up and set the phone on the table.

"The insurance company thinks someone tampered

with her brakes?" Charles paced around the kitchen. "When could that have happened?"

Someone from forensics rushed into the kitchen, "We found something. Blood on the porch swing and evidence of a scuffle."

# CHAPTER 35

Snipes showered, stepped into a clean pair of jeans, and pulled on the flannel lined denim jacket and the new pair of boots he'd bought for the trip. *Cleaned up and ready to roll.*

It was early. He hadn't slept in almost twenty-four hours but he wanted to make it to the border. Cheyenne would be a good place to get some shut-eye, check the route he'd marked on his well-worn maps, and search the Internet for places to live in Banff.

He lifted the heavy duffel over his shoulder after stuffing in the last payment he ever intended to earn from criminal activity, then made a last sweep of the trailer.

"Lake Louise!" He smiled, removing the single dog-eared post card from the front of the refrigerator, and brought it to his lips. "Lake Louise, it's been a long time. I'm comin' home."

He grabbed his keys and cell phone, tossed the phone on the floor, and smashed it with his boot. The sim card held up to the beating, so he snatched it up and flushed it down the toilet.

With a bounce in his step, he opened the rickety door of the trailer for the last time, and let it slam behind him. An odd calm spread warmly through him as he ran a hand lovingly over his new ride, buckled up, and maneuvered cautiously through the rundown part of town.

"No time for traffic tickets this morning. No sir. Goin' home."

Snipes cranked up the radio as he passed the old bowling alley and saw fire trucks, and several dozen vehicles, parked out front.

He saluted and said out loud, "Good riddance," then headed north on I-25, tapping his thumbs on the steering wheel to the beat of the music.

# CHAPTER 36

Dani's breath hitched when the upbeat tempo of Charles's unique ringtone broke the eerie silence. *Charles!* She tried to scoot the chair toward the light on her phone but her feet were so tightly secured to the wheelbase they wouldn't budge.

Five seconds... Ten... Fifteen... Twenty... Silence.

Five seconds... Ten... Fifteen... Twenty... Silence.

A minute or two passed before the ringtone began again. But after only ten seconds, bone-chilling quiet fused with the darkness again. *Dark. So dark.* Tears streamed down her cheeks and her nose was running. *Charles, do you know where I am? Find me!*

*What was that?* Something was moving in the shadows. Twisting in the chair she could just make out a tiny gray mouse staring at her through shining eyes. She moved as much as she could, which wasn't much, and she heard it scamper away.

The din of traffic began to flow more steadily on the interstate located alongside her lonely prison. *Morning. Stay calm. It can't be much longer.*

Minutes seemed like hours. She was exhausted. Her eyes drooped shut, and her head slowly fell to her chest. Pain seized her neck and shoulders, jerking her out of a sleepy haze, and she let out a muffled cry. *I can't feel my fingers.* She couldn't hold back the flood of tears any longer. *Charles!*

The sound was unmistakable. Tires–big tires–rolling over pavement. The rhythmic knocking of a diesel engine grew louder, came closer. Then another. And another.

Elation filled her heart, stopping the flow of tears. *Fire trucks! They're here!*

Muffled voices came closer, until she was sure they were right outside the room, on the other side of the wall. She worked desperately to get the chair moving toward the voices. Car doors slammed, and more voices joined the conversation, murmuring in excitement.

*No!* The chorus was moving away from her.

Jerking back and forth, forcefully, painfully, screams gurgling in her throat. *I'm in here! I'm right here! Come back, please!*

The excited voices became louder again, sounding

almost festive. Glass was breaking in the next room, and she could hear dozens of people right on the other side of the door.

Dani rocked back and forth violently, until she managed to get the chair moving toward the door. She rolled only about six inches before debris stalled her forward motion. Somehow she had to make enough noise to alert them.

Someone outside had a bullhorn. "Okay all volunteers, gather 'round so you can hear. First, all of us in the fire and rescue department would like to thank everyone who volunteered for this emergency drill. Members of our team will be rescuing volunteers under near-actual conditions. That means it might get a little scary in here, but every rescuer participating in this drill is experienced."

"We'll be conducting the drills in two phases. The first phase will be victim rescue, the second will be fire fighting. These drills are designed to closely mimic real emergency situations, therefore the only exceptions to keeping things real will be blankets for you to lay on, and breathing apparatus's, which you will all be fitted with to assure none of our volunteers ends up with smoke inhalation. So, depending on the roles you're playing, feel free to moan and groan as if you were truly injured."

"Don't worry, we don't intend to move to phase two and light up the building until everyone has been evacuated.

The masks are an extra precaution."

"Are there any questions? No? Are you all ready? Okay then, everyone grab a blanket and line up for your breathing apparatus. After that, move to the positions assigned on the map, and get into character for the rolls you've been given on the notecards."

Dani could hear people shuffling so close she felt like she could reach out and touch them if it weren't for the wall and locked door separating them.

She replayed the last conversation she had with her abductor.

*You're going to kill me, aren't you?*

*No Need.*

A horrible realization shook her. *He knew about the drill! He means for me to choke to death on smoke or worse, burn to death!*

Anguished screams burned in her throat. She writhed in the chair like a caged wild animal, attempting to loosen the ropes. *Noooooo!*

What little noise she made was drowned out by the activities in the next room. A crowd cheered outside from time to time, and the irony of saving of people who didn't really need to be rescued caused thick waves of nausea to churn in her stomach. She thought she would throw up but she willed that from happening, and drew from every ounce of strength she had left.

*No one can hear me now. Wait for the right time.*

An agonizing two hours must have passed before she heard the announcement on a bullhorn outside. "Thank you. All volunteers are accounted for, and you all made great victims."

Applause.

"Okay, we're ready to light up the building and, though we swept the building for anything explosive yesterday afternoon, we need everyone to stand behind the tape Lieutenant Goldman put up for your safety."

*Noooooo! I'm right here!*

*This is it. I have to make some noise. Now!*

Using every ounce of strength she had left, Dani managed to move up and down enough to make a faint noise with the wheels of the chair, but she couldn't hear anyone coming closer.

*Whumpf!* The unmistakable rumble of igniting fire reverberated through the building.

Terror seized her as she choked back tears, violently rocking the chair back and forth, desperately trying to hit the door hard enough to make some noise.

Pain seared through her entire body when she finally toppled, head first into the door. She could hear crackling flames moving closer, and sobbed until she lost her fight for consciousness.

*I'm alone. No one is coming.*

# CHAPTER 37

Snipes read the green highway sign out loud, "Fifteen miles to the Wyoming border then I can grab some breakfast."

Rattling off plans, sometimes in his head, sometimes out loud to himself, helped take his mind off his growling stomach. "I need a dog." He said, nodding his head to the music on the radio. "Soon as I find a place, I'm gettin' a dog. A big dog. We'll walk around Lake Louise together. Man's best friend. Yeah."

Another sign. "Wyoming two miles. Woot!"

Snipes pressed his foot a little heavier on the gas pedal, and cringed when he passed a Highway Patrol car parked on the north side of I-25. A siren blared, and the patrol car pulled in fast behind him, riding close to his bumper.

He could see the sign in the short distance ahead, "Welcome to Wyoming." Snipes stomped on the gas and just as he did, an unmarked Highway Patrol car spun its tires in the gravel median, lights and sirens blazing, and pulled in right in front of him.

Trapped, nowhere to go, Snipes slowed to a stop, turned the key in the ignition, and placed his hands on the steering wheel.

The patrolmen walked cautiously toward him, guns drawn and pointed. "Keep your hands where we can see them, and slowly step out of the car."

Snipes obeyed. "Was I speeding, officers? I'm sorry, I was hungry and I saw…"

"Alistair Snipes, you are under arrest. Face the front of the vehicle and place your hands on the hood."

"Hey! What's this about? What'd I do?"

"We'll start with driving eighty in a seventy five mile an hour speed zone. Add to that a nice big bundle of charges from Denver, and top it off with kidnapping. That about wraps it up."

"Listen," Snipes tried to reason with them, but they were busy patting him down and cuffing him "I mighta been speedin', but there's been a mistake. Hey, don't take my word for it, check out my car. You won't find anybody in there, and you'll have to let me go."

"Mr. Snipes, we're highway patrolmen, and we don't take orders from you. You're going to jail." The officers walked him to the patrol car behind his, opened the back door, eased him inside, and closed the door.

Snipes admired their calm. No theatrics, no argument, and apparently no hurry.

While the patrolman called in the details, Snipes stared straight ahead at the sign not three hundred feet in front of him. "Welcome to Wyoming." *So close.*

"We got him. Which precinct? I'm on my way."

# CHAPTER 38

The forensics team drove away in their van, leaving Charles with Terrell and Collins.

*Dani, where are you?* The words repeated over, and over in his head until he thought he might go crazy. He paced up and down the stairs, in and out of her study, and paced circles around the yard, looking for clues. When he rounded the corner–exhausted, Terrell was shouting on his radio.

"Dispatch a squad car to that location. *Now!* Alert fire and rescue immediately. We're on our way."

"Charles! Come on; get in. We found her cell phone at the old bowling alley!"

Charles was on their heels, robe flying out behind him, his heart pounding. "Bowling alley? Is she working? Is she covering the story?" He climbed into the back of the unmarked car, not sure whether to allow relief to soak through his aching head, or ramp up his panic. He hoped with his entire being she was with James, and forgot to tell him.

Collins was behind the wheel, speeding through the usually peaceful streets of Washington Park. Someone announced over the radio, "Search in progress. Building on fire."

Yanking his phone from the pocket of his robe he dialed, "Come on Dani, answer your phone." Voicemail. He redialed her number, over and over. "Damn it Dani, answer your phone!" He saw Terrell watching him, but he didn't care. The only thing that mattered to him now was finding his wife.

"Maybe James picked her up, and they're covering the story. Maybe she's not missing. Maybe she's just busy."

"We'll be there shortly, my friend. We'll find her." Terrell said.

Charles understood the words were meant to be comforting, but what he saw in Terrell's face was fear.

The speeding police car headed toward a plume of smoke billowing high into the morning sky.

"Dani won't be happy about that pollution." As soon as he said it, he knew it sounded ridiculous, but he tried to latch onto anything normal. Anything that might mean his wife was having a typical day at work.

Collins turned on the siren, clearing a space through the crowded parking lot. Several news stations were on site. Reporters interviewed spectators. Enormous cameras were rigged on tripods, and Charles scanned them, looking for James.

"There! James is right there! James!" He shouted and bumped against the car door to open it, but he was locked in. When Terrell released him, Charles bolted toward James, calling out, "James! James!"

"Hi Charles? Where's Dani?" James gave him a perplexed look, and it dawned on him how he must look, standing there in his robe, and sneakers.

His heart sank to the bottom of his stomach. "She's not with you?"

"Charles? What's wrong? She said she'd meet me here, but she never showed."

A sickening chill ran through him when he heard gasps rippling through the crowd. Some of them pointed toward the flaming building. Gleeful chatter turned to hushed exchanges.

Cameras began snapping wildly. The press rushed forward, and James snatched his camera and tripod, running toward the burning building. James shouted, "Oh my God! Someone was in there!"

Dizzy with confusion, Charles searched for Terrell and Collins. "What's happening?"

Someone on a bullhorn ordered, "Everybody stay back. This is not a drill. I repeat. This is not a drill. All volunteers have been accounted for. Give us room. Stay back."

Charles stood on his toes, craning his neck to see

someone, bound and gagged, being carried out of the burning building, tied to a chair.

Two firemen wearing heavy gear carried the chair near the back of the ambulance, and set it down gently. Paramedics supported the bobbing head with a cervical collar, and cut away black fabric. A fireman kneeled and released feet from the ropes, while another bent over to release dangling arms.

*Dani's pajamas!* Relief that they'd found her was fleeting. Realization flooded Charles with horror. His eyes were riveted on the scene.

"Dani!" His heart-wrenching scream pierced through the commotion.

The crowd turned its attention on him when he bolted, pushing anyone who got in his way. "Oh, my God, Dani!"

Terrell reached out and held him back, just a few steps from the person he loved most in this world. "Give them a minute, Charles."

Paramedics started an I.V., carefully removed the battered cast from her arm, and replaced it with a hard plastic splint. After working on her for about ten minutes, she was strapped to a gurney and loaded into the ambulance wearing an oxygen mask. She was unconscious.

Charles fought ferociously when they tried to move him to the front of the ambulance. "I'm not leaving her."

"Sir, it's policy–for safety. You can ride up front."

The muscles in his jaw rippled. "Forget it. I'm not

leaving her." He pulled away and climbed into the back of the ambulance.

Terrell whispered to the paramedics. They nodded, shut the door, and sped off.

# CHAPTER 39

The trip to New York had been a whirlwind of broadcasts, and meetings. Excited well-wishers gathered at every venue, many with tears in their eyes, thrusting contribution checks into her hands.

Mona gave each major network an exclusive on a different fundraising activity, assuring each of them had something to get behind and support. She understood the importance of network buy-in; it meant free airtime for the foundation.

Her marketing department, energized by the enthusiasm, stayed two steps ahead of her. They developed fresh ideas and activities on the fly, making sure the appropriate apparel made it to each studio in time for on-air distribution to the press.

By the time she boarded the plane for L.A., the excitement in New York had reached a crescendo.

Jackie reported that phone calls, and contributions, exceeded their most hopeful expectations. The message was hope. The masses were hungry for it.

"Mona, wait 'til you hear about the first activity for California. Volleyball tournaments! We have the backing of fifteen Olympic hopefuls. That will go over big in L.A."

"Volleyball! That's brilliant. Arrange a catered lunch for the marketing department, will you dear?"

"Of course. Anything else, Mona?" Jackie asked.

"I haven't heard from Todd. Is he on his way to L.A.?"

"Yes, he called from the airport. He said he'll meet you at the hotel."

"Thank you, Jackie. I'll check in again soon. Bye."

Mona smiled at the flight attendant who offered warm, lemon scented towels, and asked what she'd like to drink. Settling back in her comfortable first-class seat she ordered wine and Brie.

An hour into the flight, the pleasant woman who'd served her earlier slid into the empty seat beside Mona. "I hope I'm not intruding, but I wanted to thank you for everything you do for women, Ms. Davenport. Your campaigns are always so much fun, and the services you provide, the chemotherapy drugs you've funded..." The woman swiped at a tear before it fell.

Mona reached out and patted her hand. "Battling this horrible disease is my life's work, dear. I wouldn't know what else to do with my time. The American Pink Ribbon Foundation is as much as gift to me as it is to the women, and men, we assist. Has breast cancer touched you in some way?"

"Yes, it has. I'm a four-year survivor, and I'm so grateful to be alive. My sister and I participate in your annual event in Chicago every year, and we'll continue until we either fall over dead, or you manage to wipe out this awful disease. It's a devastating diagnosis; the treatment is barbaric but…" she choked back tears, "Here I am."

The woman regained her composure, and continued. "I saw you on TV yesterday. I dread to think I might pass this along to my daughter. Or, that my sister, or nieces might develop it someday. Do you really believe you can develop a vaccine to prevent breast cancer?"

"I'm quite confident in the research team at Diaxler Pharmaceuticals. With the help of our supporters, I hope to fully fund their research over the coming years. My only regret is that we didn't understand sooner that a virus could be the culprit."

"I sure hope you're right, Ms. Davenport." The flight attendant stood up, pulled an envelope from her pocket, and placed it on Mona's dining tray. "God bless you."

Mona spotted Todd in the lobby of the Four Seasons Los Angeles, reading the Denver Tribune. "Todd, dear. I do hope I haven't kept you waiting long."

"Not at all. I just checked in." Todd stood up and pointed to the New York Times sitting on the coffee table. "From what I've read, you stirred up quite a frenzy in New York. I hope we can do the same in L.A. The talk show circuit is new to me, but you seem to be in your element."

"Thank you, Todd. I do enjoy it. Jackie tells me contributions have reached record highs."

Todd nodded. "Excellent. Your room key is waiting for you at the desk. Why don't I let you settle in while I make reservations for dinner?"

"That sounds lovely, Todd. Give me a couple of hours, will you? I want to get a massage before dinner."


They were seated at the posh Providence restaurant in L.A. at precisely nine p.m. "The food and service here are said to be impeccable." Todd said. "The concierge recommended the cheese tray, and said to save room for at least a bite of dessert."

Mona studied him for a moment. "Todd, you look tired. You really should have had a massage; it's so relaxing. I hope our schedule isn't causing your fatigue." She noticed a change in him. He was adept at turning on the charm when necessary, and most people would never have noticed anything different in him. But she had worked on many projects with this man for almost twelve years, and she could read him well.

"Of course not," he said. "I'll admit, there are a million details, and some of them are proving more difficult to manage that I expected. But, I can assure you our collaboration will be a masterpiece. One we can both retire on."

Mona picked up her wine glass and proposed a toast. "To our collaboration."

When he raised his glass, Mona noticed his bandage. "Todd, dear. What happened to your hand?"

"It's nothing." He smirked. "One of those little details is all."

"Do take care of yourself." She said. "And speaking of details–you mentioned hacking into that nasty little Driscoll blog. Were you successful?"

"I was. There is no more blog; it's gone. Poof!" He said it with a flick of his hand.

"Good. She was in my office the day I left for New York, making all kinds of insinuations. I don't know where that girl gets her information. You'd think a reporter would have better instincts."

"Mona, you have plenty to do without worrying about a silly little reporter. I told you a month ago to leave her to me. I admit to making a slight miscalculation, and I was close to eliminating that particular problem." Todd stuck a fork into a piece of cheese and waived it at her. "But, she's more resilient than I gave her credit for. I won't make the same mistake again."

Mona's pulse quickened. She topped off her wine glass, staring at him. "What did you do?"

"The less you know, the better." He said.

Todd ran his thumb back and forth over his bandaged hand, and leaned in closer. "Now listen carefully. You and I have a ten-year plan to rake in all the dough we can. We need to milk this for all it's worth. Apparently it's worth more than we thought in our wildest dreams. After this is finished, we'll go our separate ways; retire in grand style. I'm thinking Monte Carlo, myself."

For the first time in her life, Mona was deeply frightened. This man whom she thought she knew, looked like a madman to her in the candlelight.

He skewered a piece of rare steak. "So, don't you worry about that pesky reporter; I've swept that little detail under the carpet alongside Dr. Nolan Jennings, and his annoying research. We're in the spotlight now. I plan to stay in it."

# CHAPTER 40

Charles stood, rocking from one foot to the other, staring out the window, and twisting his wedding band. The ICU waiting room was filled with friends, but he had nothing to say to any of them. He refused the coffee they brought. He wasn't interested in the bagels or muffins they offered. All he wanted in the world was to see his wife's beautiful smile.

He replayed the events of the past twelve hours over and over in his head, until he was nauseous and exhausted.

*Who would do this to her? Everyone loves her; why would anyone want to harm my wife?*

He knew the reason in his gut. *I begged her to let this go. Why, Dani?*

"Mr. Driscoll?" An ICU nurse was standing in the doorway.

He snapped to attention. "Yes, I'm here."

The nurse smiled at him. "She's asking for you."

He rounded the corner to her room, assessing the surroundings as he hurried toward her. Oxygen, IV's, EKG leads, beeping machines measuring every beat, every breath. He was startled when he saw her bandaged head. Her lovely face was bruised, her eyes barely open through the swelling. Her lips were dry and cracked.

She looked battered but he didn't want to upset her, so composed himself the best he could. "Hi Sweetheart." His lips quivered a little, and he willed himself to be strong, swallowing hard before he continued. "How are you feeling?"

Recognition registered in her eyes, then they fluttered, and closed. Her breathing was shallow, and Charles flashed the nurse an alarmed look.

"She's tired. It's a good sign that she asked for you." The nurse's words were only slightly comforting.

Charles took his wife's hand, examining the cuts and bruises on her wrist. Remembering the chair she was tied to, he gently pulled back the sheet and saw rope marks and cuts on her ankles.

"Charles?" It was barely a whisper.

He quickly wiped a tear from his face, and smiled at her. "Yes I'm here, Sweetheart. Looks like you've a rough day." He stroked her cheek.

"I wish I could tell you the other guy looks worse, but..." Her voice was weak, and she tried to smile, but grimaced instead. "No."

"Terrell got him, Dani. The guy's in custody. He won't be causing you, or anyone else, any harm. Knowing Terrell, he'll make sure this guy goes to prison with no chance of getting out."

She smiled through swollen lips. "Can I have some water?"

"I'm not sure. I'll ask a nurse." He pressed the button tied to the sidebar of the hospital bed, and a nurse arrived immediately, with a doctor on her heels.

The doctor answered her question. "You can have water, and a soft diet until ten p.m. How do you feel about Jell-O?"

"Jell-O's good." She replied in a hoarse voice. "Throat hurts."

The doctor nodded. "From smoke inhalation. You have a concussion, and we'll watch that closely, but I intend to have you in surgery bright and early in the morning."

"Surgery? What's wrong with me?"

"You have multiple fractures of both bones in your left forearm, a hairline fracture in your upper arm, and a fractured wrist. The bones in your forearm were shattered and we need to put in a steel plate and some screws."

"I still have those in my left knee, from a car accident." Dani said.

The doctor nodded, and continued. "We're watching you for signs of internal injuries, but I think we're okay there.

Our main concern is the concussion. Your husband here has been anxious to see you. How do you feel?"

"Headache." She sipped some water through a straw. "I hurt all over."

"I'm not surprised. You had a couple of good knocks to the head, and we've stitched up the gash in your forehead. We have you on antibiotics and, as for being sore I'll be honest. You're in for a rough few weeks. Right now, your job is to rest."

"Can you put that in writing, doctor? My wife's a pretty stubborn woman." Charles managed a weak smile.

The doctor peered over his glasses, and looked at her sternly. "If necessary."

His expression became sympathetic. "Mrs. Driscoll, you've been through a traumatic experience. I've ordered a consult with the hospital psychologist. I think it's wise, under the circumstances."

Charles nodded. "I think that's a good idea."

She nodded, closed her eyes and swallowed. "I'll cooperate in any way I can. I remember... I remember." She opened her eyes, and a tear slid down her cheek. "That man is a monster. If you ask me, he's the one who needs the psych visit."

Her lips quivered, and she started to tremble. One of the monitors alarmed, and the doctor reached over, and quieted it.

Charles wrapped her in his arms as best he could without dislodging the monitors. "Shhhh, shhhhh, I've got you Sweetheart."

The doctor started toward the door. "I'm going to order something to help calm you." He hesitated, "Do you feel safe here, Dani?"

"Yes. I know I'm safe here. I just... He..."

In spite of what she said, Charles could see fear in her swollen eyes. He gently wiped away the tears that streamed over her cheeks.

The doctor nodded. "Remember, your foremost job is to rest as much as possible. I'll tell the detective in the waiting room he has to wait."

"Terrell?" She tried to sit up straighter.

"I'll go look." Charles kissed her hand. "But I'm not leaving. I'll be right back."

The next thing she heard was, "Hey Dani-girl." Terrell had a big grin on his face. "It's good to see you awake. I was beginning to think you were gonna sleep the whole day away."

"Terrell, you look awful."

Charles looked at Terrell, and the two of them laughed.

"What?" She sipped some water. "Honestly, you both look awful. I think that doctor needs to give the two of you something to relax."

Her tone turned serious; tears welled up and spilled over. "Charles said you caught the man who tied me up, and left me for dead. How did you catch him so fast?"

"Thanks to your persistence, we got the clues we needed from that old clunker. We cracked the case with that one clue. Fingerprints were everywhere. We questioned the dealership, and got his name in quick order. The manager told us what he was driving and I issued an APB for him, and for you. It turned out he was easier to find."

"Charles here, has been a mess. Seems to me you hold up a little better under pressure, Dani-girl."

"I'm sorry I got myself into this situation. You both tried to warn me to let this go. I guess I'll pay more attention the next time someone says I need to pipe down."

They both rolled their eyes.

"So sleepy." she said.

"You need your rest. But first, if you can manage, I'd like you to take a look at some photos." Terrell reached in his pocket, and unfolded a single sheet of paper. "The case is tight but an ID from you would put a nice lid on it. I don't want to upset you, though. Do you think you can handle it, Dani?"

She nodded, and took the sheet of paper with six identically sized photos precisely arranged on it.

Charles noticed her grimace as she narrowed her eyes to focus on the men in the photos, then glance around the room looking from the photos to Terrell, to Charles, then back to Terrell.

"I wish I could see the eyes better." She said.

"Which photo?" Terrell asked.

"All of them. I really don't think..." Confusion turned to recognition when she held the paper at arm's length. "Um... Charles, this looks like your jacket. See the missing button?"

"How the..." Eyes wide, he turned to Terrell. "He was in the house, in our bedroom?"

Dani continued. "There's only one problem."

"What is it Dani-girl?"

"None of these is the man who abducted me."

# CHAPTER 41

Alistair Snipes fidgeted with the handcuffs, and looked at the wall behind Terrell and Collins while they interrogated him.

Terrell repeated, "Alistair, are you sure you don't want an attorney? We have all the evidence we need to put you away for a very long time."

Snipes blinked nervously. "I told you. I wasn't speedin', and I never kidnapped anybody in my whole life. You don't have nuthin' on me."

"I think we have quite a lot, to be honest. For starters, where did you get the denim jacket you were wearing when they brought you in?" Terrell analyzed his body language. He studied Snipes' every move, and expression.

"Don't know." His fingers tapped on the table.

"You don't know? Well, let's see if you know the answer to my next question. Those are fresh scratches on your face, Alistair. Your eye is bloodshot. What happened? You get in a fight with someone?"

Snipes snickered. "Name's Snipes. Call me Snipes. I was movin' outta my trailer-house, and ran into a tree branch is all." His mouth appeared to be dry when he spoke.

"I see." Terrell pushed, "And what about the money? Most people don't carry that kind of cash around. Where did the money come from?"

"That's my life savings. I got my life savings with me 'cause I was movin' to Canada. Nothing wrong with that, is there?"

"No," Collins reasoned. "Since you're not on parole, there isn't anything wrong with taking your life savings, and moving to Canada. But I still see a problem."

"Yeah?" Snipes replied sarcastically. "I see a problem, too. I should be halfway across Wyoming by now."

Collins continued. "The problem I see is this. In order for your relocation to be legal, the money you're taking with you can't be tied to a crime. Where did you get the money, Alistair?"

He rolled his eyes. "I told you to call me Snipes. Nobody's called me Alistair since my mom died."

Terrell slammed his fist down hard on the table just inches from Snipes' cuffed hands. "Where did you get the money?"

Snipes sneered, and chuckled "Well, I didn't rob a

bank, if that's what you're gettin' at. Not that I ain't smart enough. I could, ya know. But I guarantee that money's not from any bank heist." He sat back in his chair, apparently pleased with himself.

Terrell pushed harder. "We know the money's not from a bank robbery, and we know you didn't save that kind of money working as a fork lift operator. In fact, before you went to prison you were flat broke according to your file. Who are you working for, Alistair?"

His eyes darted toward the ceiling, and he shook his head. "How many times do I have to tell you to call me Snipes?"

Terrell leaned across the table. "Okay Snipes. How can you explain obtaining almost a quarter of a million dollars since you were released from prison? Convince me you earned it. Who did you work for? A simple phone call could clear up any misunderstanding, and a lot of these charges along with it."

Snipes was defiant. "It's none of your business how I made that money, but I can tell you I earned every last dollar. It wasn't easy, either, and I want it back. It's mine."

"Really, Mr. Snipes?" Collins spread her hands on the table. "I'm afraid it is our business. Look, we have you on some major charges. Vehicular homicide, hit and run, breaking and entering, and theft for starters. And we suspect you were involved in a kidnapping. But what we're really interested in right now is who you're working for."

"You don't have nuthin' on me, and you know it. I work for myself. I'm what you call self employed." Snipes nodded proudly.

Terrell leaned in close to Snipes, and looked him straight in the eyes. He slowly pushed himself up from the table, and left the room. He returned carrying the laptop taken into evidence from the Ford Escape, and pushed it across the table toward the suspect. "Snipes, where did you get this?"

"Craigslist." Snipes swallowed hard, sweat was beading on his forehead.

Terrell pulled a boxed pen and pencil set out of his pocket, set it down on the table, and opened it. "And did you get this from Craigslist, too?"

His face went white. "I'm not sayin' anymore 'til I get somethin' to eat. I got money to pay for it. Just take it outta my duffel bag."

"That money is evidence. In fact, your vehicle, and everything in it, is evidence now. That means you can't even buy a two dollar steak." Terrell motioned for Collins to get him a sandwich.

"Snipes, do you mind if we chat, man to man, while we wait for your lunch?"

Snipes shrugged, raising his handcuffed hands. "Why not? I got nothin' else to do."

"I have a lot of respect for anyone who has the guts to work for himself. It can't be easy getting jobs, keeping the money coming in. You're obviously good at what you do."

"That's right, I am good." Snipes thrust out his chest, and pulled his shoulder back.

"Me? I'm just working for a paycheck, day after day, week after week. I'll be lucky if I can save that kind of money in my lifetime on what I make. Yet you've made all that money in a matter of months." Terrell placed his hands, palms up on the table in front of Snipes. "I'm just wondering, after all that work, making all that money, and planning your trip to Canada... Why not cut a deal for leniency? All you have to do is tell me whom you're working for. I'll put in a good word with the judge for you."

"Look, I ain't afraid to go back to prison. Three squares a day, a bed, rent-free. It ain't all bad, ya know. I had some good friends in there. Learned a lot, too."

Terrell nodded. "I can understand that. But you'll never get to Canada now."

Collins returned with a sandwich, and a soft drink from the vending machine. She dropped the sandwich in front of him. "Here you go, Mr. Snipes. Lunch is served."

Terrell laid a hand over the sandwich wrapped in plastic. "Snipes, this is my last offer to work a deal. Whom are you working for?"

Snipes eyed the sandwich, and sneered. "I'll take that

lawyer now if we're gonna be here all day."

Terrell stood up and nodded for the public defender. Before he left the room with Collins he turned to Snipes. "Just answer one question for me, Snipes. Were you working for a woman?"

Snipes threw his head back, and laughed. "A woman? I don't answer to any woman. No bitch is ever gonna tell me what to do."

Terrell wound his way through the police station, and slammed his way through the side door with Collins close on his heels. "Damnit!"

He paced back and forth. "Damnit, damnit, damnit!"

Collins held out an arm. "Stop. I know you're upset. We'll get the bastard who kidnapped Dani."

Terrell slouched against the wall. "But it's not him."

Collins stood with her hands on her hips. "No. It's not Snipes. But we knew that when she failed to identify the photos you showed her. She specifically stated none of those photos was him, and he doesn't match the body type description, either."

"That means her kidnapper is still at large, and I'm still convinced there's a connection to Snipes. I feel it in my gut." He tapped a fist to his stomach. "Dani may not be an investigative reporter, but she's a smart woman who's apparently knocked over someone's cookie jar. These cases are all connected somehow, and I know the money in that duffel is the common link. It has to be. We know Snipes was in the Driscoll residence."

"That car was seen at two crime scenes, and he had the Jennings computer in his vehicle. He'll talk when we book him on murder one." Collins said.

Snipes sat in his cell, playing the conversation over and over in his head.

*Now listen carefully.* The voice had been menacing; like some of the meanest guys in prison. *I can't be connected to you, even if you're caught. You're paid very well to complete the tasks given to you, and if there are consequences to your actions, then the consequences are yours. Do we understand each other?*

*I'd be a dead man in a week. That guy's mean as a snake.*

# CHAPTER 42

Terrell and Collins knocked on the door of the Jennings residence, and were greeted warmly by Suzanne.

"Detectives, come in." She opened the door, and led them to the family room. "Can I get you a beverage?"

She took a plate from the kitchen cabinet and nervously began arranging cookies. "Dolores from next door brought over a fresh baked batch of oatmeal cookies just this morning." She set the plate in from of them with a stack of napkins. "Please help yourselves."

Suzanne sat down on the edge of a chair and smoothed her skirt. "I assume you have news on the robbery. Did you find Nolan's things?" Her lip quivered slightly and she caught her bottom lip in her teeth.

Terrell replied, "Yes, Mrs. Jennings. We found your husband's laptop, and we have a suspect in custody."

She closed her eyes and took in a long, hitching breath. "That's wonderful news, Detectives. I appreciate your diligence. You only found the laptop? Nothing else?"

Terrell continued. "We've only recovered the laptop, and a pen and pencil set at this time. But I'm afraid there's more, Mrs. Jennings. This isn't going to be easy to hear."

Collins shot him a warning look he was familiar with. *Be gentle.*

Terrell nodded, and continued. "We have reason to believe the vehicle used in the burglary was also the vehicle that hit your husband." He paused to assess Suzanne's reaction.

She looked directly at him with a furrowed brow, slowly shaking her head as if she was trying to comprehend what she'd just been told. An enormous silence filled the room, and Collins looked as though she was ready to dive for the box of tissues on the end table.

"A coincidence?" She whispered hopefully.

Collins lowered her voice. "No, we don't think so, Mrs. Jennings."

She slumped back in the chair momentarily, smoothing her skirt over and over. "No!" She sat up stick-straight, and denied the news emphatically. "You're implying Nolan was…" Suzanne's composure dissolved. She shook her head violently. "No, that's not possible. No one would hurt Nolan. He was gentle, kind, loving."

"And a gifted researcher, if I'm not mistaken," Collins said.

Suzanne looked at her with wide eyes, and whispered. "Yes. Yes, he was. Gifted in many ways."

"Mrs. Jennings, do you know of anyone who might have been jealous of your husband's accomplishments? Do you remember him receiving any threats?" Terrell asked.

Her eyes searched the ceiling. "No one. Nolan always shared credit with his colleagues. He got along with everyone, he was so easy-going." Her voice trailed off, and she chewed on her bottom lip and wrung her hands.

After a moment, Suzanne slid back to the edge the chair. "Detectives, I'm sorry, I'm confused. Didn't you say you have someone in custody?"

Terrell answered. "We do. We found some of the items that fit the description from the boxes Dr. McCleary delivered to you, and the laptop. The items were in the suspect's vehicle along with quite a lot of cash. What we don't have on him is a motive."

"Who!" She demanded, her voice shaking. "Who is it?"

Collins reached for Suzanne's hand. "His name is Alistair Snipes. We're holding him on a number of charges."

Suzanne shook her head. "I've never heard that name before."

Collins handed Suzanne a tissue for the tears that rolled down her cheeks. "No, we didn't think you had, Mrs.

Jennings. We still have work to do on this case, but we didn't want you to hear about this on the news."

"I appreciate that, Detectives."

Terrell stood up and held out a business card. "If you remember anything that might be helpful, please call me anytime, day or night."

She nodded, started toward the door with them, and stopped. "Wait! Are my husband's colleagues in danger? If you really think this is about Nolan's work... They're good people, detective Holt. They're carrying on in Nolan's name. Do you think they're safe?"

"Yes, I believe they are." Collins answered. "We have a suspect in custody, and the department is working the case around the clock."

Collins reached for the door and hesitated. "I believe you're safe, too, Mrs. Jennings."

Suzanne nodded.

When they closed the door behind them, Terrell and Collins could hear her sobbing.

# CHAPTER 43

Charles and Coop were hovering over the hospital bed when she woke up from surgery. She tried to focus her eyes on the new cast covering most of her left arm. Her fingers felt thick and stiff when she tried to wiggle them.

"Wake up sleepy head. How are you?" Charles leaned over and kissed her.

"Mmmmm. I was sleeping so good." Dani blinked slowly, and looked around the unfamiliar room. "I'm not in ICU anymore. That's good."

Charles nodded. "It is good. Everything went as expected and the doctor said you might be able to go home in two or three days."

"Two or three days! Wanna bet I can talk him into letting me out of here tomorrow?"

"There's the mischievous grin I love." He looked at her

lovingly, and teased, "Well, don't expect me to back you up this time. As long as you're here, I'll know you're behaving."

She let her sleepy gaze turn to Coop, and said quietly, "I guess you know the whole story by now. I'm sorry I went behind your back, but I'm more suspicious than ever of Mona's intentions. In fact, I have every reason to think..."

Coop looked at her with a stern, fatherly expression, and pointed his finger at her. "Your job is to get better, young lady. You can't imagine how horrified I was when I saw James's footage. I've tripled my antacids, and poor James was frantic seeing you like that."

"There's a story here, you know. Want me to write it up?" She grinned at him sleepily, and made an uncoordinated attempt to bat her eyelashes. "Nope. Too sleepy."

An enormous teddy bear floated toward her. Honey peeked around it, flashing her brilliant smile. "How's my favorite reporter?"

Charles relieved Honey of the substantial stuffed animal, and set it on the foot of her bed. He replied, "In trouble, as usual."

Dani rolled her eyes. "That's really cute, Honey. Thank you."

"My daughters insisted it was better than flowers. They overheard me talking about you to my husband, though I didn't want to upset them by saying you'd been kidnapped. I told them you were in the hospital, and they wanted to come and interview you."

"Your little girls are adorable. Tell them I said thank you, and they'll be the first to know when I'm granting interviews."

Honey continued, "ICU wouldn't let me in yesterday, since I'm not family. I've been worried since I saw your rescue on the news. They still haven't released details as to what happened, or why. Who in the world would want to kidnap you?"

"It's a long story." Dani said.

"How's your campaign coming along? Are you still planning to support the Rush research?" She caught a glimpse of the incredulous look on Charles' face.

"I am. The ads will start in the newspapers on Friday, and I just filmed the TV commercial this morning. Dr. McCleary's team is thrilled. They are the nicest, and smartest people I've ever met. Did I tell you they invited me to tour their laboratory?" Honey's eyes shone with excitement.

Coop piped in, "I saw your ads, Ms. Romano. Your ad agency does a beautiful job."

"Thank you, Coop. My goal is to raise a million dollars for Seth's research. Money is the only thing holding them back at this point, and the research thus far is conclusive. Everyone else is spending research money on toxic drugs, and that's not what I want for my daughters. I want the vaccine that prevents them from ever needing to take those drugs."

Dani saw Charles and Coop exchange concerned looks.

"I agree. Why would Mona and her drug company start over when the research has already been done?" Dani tried unsuccessfully to stifle a yawn. "I'm sorry, that was rude."

"No, no. I should be going. Promise we'll have lunch when you're able?" Honey squeezed her free hand.

"I'd love it. Thank you for stopping by, Honey."

"I'll walk out with you, Ms. Romano." Coop said.

He leaned over and planted a kiss on Dani's check. "Take care of yourself. You know you're like the daughter I never had."

She nodded. "I will. Bye Coop."

Charles busied himself with filling Dani's water container before he sat down in the chair beside her. The anguished look on his face made her heart ache.

"Sweetheart. You know I love you completely," he said.

She sensed what was coming. "I know, Charles. I love you too, with all my heart. I'm sorry my actions caused you so much worry."

She could hear the pain in his voice as he went on, taking her hand in his. "Since the moment I first saw you six years ago, I knew there was no one else for me. I knew without a shadow of a doubt that I wanted to spend the rest of my life with you. I still feel that way. My life is so intertwined with yours, all the joy in my life slipped away with you that night."

She nodded, unable to come up with the words to comfort him.

"Dani, we have a wonderful life together. I believe one of the reasons we work so well is that we communicate with each other. We dream together, plan together. It works in such a lovely way for us."

He stroked her arm. "When you pointed out that the guy in Terrell's photo was wearing my jacket, I didn't say anything. I prayed you were mistaken. You'd been through so much I didn't want to upset you. I checked our closet, Dani. My jacket is gone. That man was in our house, and that's too close for comfort."

She nodded. "Yes, it is. I was hoping it was a coincidence, too. That explains why the back door was open the night we went out for Chinese, remember? Did you notice anything else missing? Did you look through the house?"

She could tell he was weighing his words.

"Yes, I looked through the house, and I don't think anything else is missing. But that's not my point. Dani, my point is you put yourself in danger. You almost died in that fire. If not for Terrell..." He paused and shook his head. "This shook the very foundation of our relationship. Because without you, there is no us."

The anguished look on his face tore at her heart, and she struggled for the right words to comfort him. "I'm so sorry, Charles. I never looked at it from your perspective, and I should have. But, I had no idea there was danger in asking questions, and posting opinions online."

"Sweetheart, why did this have you wound so tightly you couldn't let it go? You've been a journalist for ten years, and I've never seen you dig your heels in like that. I want to understand so we can put this behind us."

Dani tried to explain. "I want the world to know that someone means to quell the biggest hope the world has ever had for stopping breast cancer in its tracks. This is a conspiracy, Charles."

"You're right. I can see now that someone is conspiring to keep the Jennings research from moving forward. Someone is obviously willing to pay a very high price to hamper its success. But the price of finding and exposing that person was very nearly your life, and that's as personal as it gets for me."

"I don't know what to say Charles." She said quietly.

"Sweetheart, I want you to say you'll walk away from this now. Your conversation with Honey has me concerned."

She lowered her head, and shrugged. "I don't know if I can walk away now." She said it as gently as she could.

Charles stood up, closed the door to her room, and sat on the side of the hospital bed with a panicked expression.

"Dani, you can't be serious. Listen to me please. Let's invite Coop to the house when you get home. Tell him what you know, what you suspect. He'll assign one of his investigative reporters to this, I'm sure of it. He can't doubt there's something here—not after seeing James's video of firemen carrying you out of a burning building."

"So you agree there is a conspiracy to keep Dr. Jennings' research out of the main stream media?" She held her breath, knowing she was treading on tender feelings.

"I can hardly dispute that now, can I? It's very clear that someone wants your silence very badly."

"Charles, a man was murdered for hoping he could prevent millions of women from getting cancer. What kind of person would I be if I turned my back on that knowledge?"

The blood rushed to his face. "Yes! Yes, I'll concede Dr. Jennings was most likely murdered. But, there isn't anything you can do about that. You can't bring him back from the dead. I don't think you realize how close to death you were yourself less than two days ago!" He was pacing now, angrier than she'd ever seen him.

"Yes, I remember, and I was terrified. But what was it all for if I don't finish what I started?"

"It is finished, Dani. Terrell has a suspect in custody. He was sick with worry when you went missing. All of us were."

"I believe he has the man who killed Dr. Jennings, but I don't believe he has the man who kidnapped me. The faces in the photos... I've tried to match them to the man who took me but it's just not him."

"Dani, it was dark—you said so yourself. And the knock on your head was hard enough to cause a concussion. I don't see how you can be sure. Who else would kidnap you, and leave you for dead? What other explanation could there be?"

# CHAPTER 44

Bridget found a space in the parking lot in time to see Seth pull up to the front door and let Amy out of his car. *They deserve some happiness.* She smiled, and waited for a moment before heading to the door, giving them time to carry out their innocent ruse.

"Good morning, Amy." She pulled on her lab coat, and peered into some of the cages. "Good morning, little ones. How is everyone this morning?"

Amy looked as though she hadn't had much sleep. "I still can't get the images out of my head of Dani Driscoll being carried out of that building tied to an office chair. It gives me nightmares. Who would do something like that? Have you heard anything else about it?"

"Only that she's going to recover. The police are being very tight-lipped about it, but I hope it's because they're busy building a case. She's such a sweet person. Remember how awkward it was the day after Nolan's accident? None of us knew what to say to her, and she did her best to put all of us at ease. I hope she's okay."

Keri stood leaning against her desk. "Me too. It didn't look good when they carried her out of there. I was afraid she wasn't going to make it."

"Good morning ladies. How are Nolan's little ones fairing today?" Seth strode in a little too nonchalantly.

Bridget smiled at him. "Seth, I think it's time to put your name on the door. The mice. The research. This is your baby now. None of us will ever forget Nolan, but you deserve to have your name on this lab going forward."

Amy beamed. "I agree."

"You are the one responsible for the research now, Seth. It's unanimous," Keri said.

"I'll order the changes." Bridget put on her glasses, and jotted a note on her "To Do" list.

Seth nodded. "All right. But, this vaccine will be known as the Jennings Breast Cancer Vaccine. None of us would be here without Nolan."

Bridget could tell he was choking back tears, so she changed the subject. "Keri, any word on funding?"

"Ugh! The only word these charitable organizations know, is "no"." I don't get it. Isn't this," Keri pointed toward the cages of mice, "the very kind of research they all claim to be supporting?"

"I've given that some thought." Bridget said. "After reading that blog, Hope Incorporated, I believe there's something more to our growing stack of rejection letters. The blogger made a good point when she said our vaccine could put them out of business."

Seth rubbed his face. "But Mona Davenport's sudden surge in popularity proves that whoever funds a successful vaccine will enjoy fame, and fortune. I see a news report about her every time I turn the channel lately. Have you seen her TV tour?"

Keri raised a finger. "I have. It's disgusting. I can tell you from first-hand experience, she's a very manipulative woman. She doesn't hear anyone's voice but her own."

Bridget nodded. "Apparently so, since she convinced you to move to Denver."

"I don't regret moving here at all. I'm so happy to be a part of this team. But, now that she's turned her back on this research and started her own campaign, I can promise you I will never participate in another of her fundraisers. She will never see as much as a penny donation from me again."

"I agree with you, Keri." Amy pulled her ponytail out of the back of her lab coat. "We need a celebrity–an ambassador. Someone who can get interviews in the press."

Bridget agreed. "That would be great but a lot of celebrities are involved with big charities already. Getting them to make a switch after they've publically supported a charity would be tough."

Keri agreed. "As nice as it sounds, I think our best chance of funding now is through a grant. The next proposal is almost finished; I'm targeting government funding now, since it's obvious to me the charitable organizations aren't interested in prevention."

# CHAPTER 45

"Déjà vu." Dani limped into the living room wearing a sling to support her arm. "Didn't I just do this?" She grinned up at her husband.

"Yes, and I hope it's the last time. Unless, of course you're ready to settle down, and start a family." Charles helped her into a chair and winked. "That's a hospital run I'd gladly make."

"Every muscle in my body aches. Don't talk to me about labor right now."

"Need something for pain?" Charles offered.

"You know I hate to take drugs. They cause too many side effects. Then the side effects are treated with a different drug, which also has side effects, ad infinitum. I'll be fine; it's not that bad. I am getting hungry though."

"The fridge is full. The neighbors saw your little TV

appearance, and delivered enough food for a month."

She cringed, and put her free hand over her face. "I wish they hadn't aired that footage."

"Take advantage of it; you're a celebrity now. No one will refuse you an interview for the next five years."

"Always a silver lining." She said." What do we have to eat?"

"Homemade soup, chicken casserole, lasagna... Or I can make sandwiches."

"Let's try the casserole and some hot tea. I think I'll check my computer while you heat it up." She stood up slowly, and headed toward her study.

A few minutes later Charles appeared in the doorway. "Lunch is served, and it smells delicious."

"It does, I can smell it from here." She looked at him with tears swimming in her eyes. "My blog is gone."

"I'm sorry, Sweetheart. I know how hard you worked on it. Do you think it can be recovered?"

"I doubt it. It's too risky, anyway. I kept all my posts in a Word document so I still have them, but any followers I had are lost."

He nodded. "What are you working on then?"

"Well, remember when I covered the debate, and tried to tell Senator Newman that breast cancer costs over fifty billion dollars a year?"

He leaned in the doorway with his arms crossed. "Yes, and as I recall, he didn't seem interested."

"He wasn't—not at all. And do you know why I think that is? I found a website last week that lists political contributions of the largest pharmaceutical companies. The drug companies spend over two million dollars a year in campaign funding."

"Big business has a lot of influence." Charles said.

"They sure do. That same website publishes background information on lobbyists. Did you know that big pharma lobbyists outnumber Congress two to one? That's a lot of power, don't you think?"

"Not surprising I guess, if you think about how many drug companies there are." He stood behind her, rubbing her shoulders.

"I also found an article about the pressure these drug lobbyists put on Congress. They even stand on the steps of the Capitol urging them to vote in favor of legislation that helps maintain their profits."

"I thought you were hungry." Charles chuckled.

She turned around slowly in her chair. "I haven't been able to investigate properly because I couldn't use my name or credentials after Coop shut me down. Writing for the Trib is the way I get my foot in the door for interviews."

"Dani, this is bigger than you, don't you see that? It's evident to me that Coop had good reason to shut you down.

He was protecting you. Sweetheart, your suspicions involve powerful people. There's inherent danger in exposing influential people, and Coop knows it."

"Exactly! But that doesn't mean they shouldn't be exposed. It doesn't mean they shouldn't be held to the same standards as the rest of society. The idea that anyone would put profits before health is disgusting."

She continued, "Mona crushed any chance of the Jennings research being funded with her expensive pink stilettos–that's very clear to me. And the reason that it's not clear to everyone else is because the press is biased toward its advertisers. This isn't right, Charles."

"Dani, you just got home from the hospital. Why are you getting wound up about this again?"

She sucked in a deep breath and held it for a moment. "Charles, I've been thinking about something, and I want to discuss it with you because I realize now how important communication is in our relationship."

"Go on." Charles took in a long slow breath, and let it out.

"I've been working in the same job for ten years. I love it, but it's easy for me now. I feel like I've stayed in my comfort zone too long. There's nothing challenging about what I do. Pete is right–I write fluff. But digging into the details of Dr. Jennings' accident, which is apparently a murder... Charles, I'm excited about journalism again."

"You're not thinking about resigning from the Trib, are you?" He furrowed his brow.

"No. I want to talk to Coop about transitioning to investigative reporting. My first assignment could be investigating the link between politicians, and drug companies."

Charles looked at her with a pleading expression. "Sweetheart, you can't be serious. You've experienced first hand how dangerous that can be. This investigation into the Jennings' murder turned our lives upside down, and nearly got you killed."

"But, Charles don't you see? I'm the reason the police knows there was a murder. I'm proud of that. The problems I encountered were because I wasn't on assignment. I couldn't use my credentials to get real interviews. I was working incognito—even my blog was anonymous. With the Trib behind me, I really think I could be good at this." Her eyes glistened with the excitement she felt.

Charles shook his head, and tried unsuccessfully to stifle a smile. "The work hours would be unpredictable, and long."

"Yes." Butterflies swirled in her stomach. She knew she was ready for this, but she wanted his blessing before she pitched it to Coop.

"Let's have lunch and talk about it some more." He helped her up, and she limped to the kitchen.

Dani watched two rabbits scurry across the yard and stop just outside the kitchen window to munch some brown grass. She slipped her cast out of the sling, and rested it on the table.

"I love this house." She said. "Our kitchen. Our yard. Aren't you glad we ended up here?"

"I'm glad we ended up living across the street from Terrell. I shudder to think what might have happened to you if he hadn't shown up here that morning."

She nodded. "I know. I owe him big, and I have no idea how to thank him. He's a good detective and a good friend."

"I don't supposed you'd consider re-paying him by opening up a bakery, would you?" Charles set a cup of tea in front of her.

Dani leaned over the steaming cup, letting the fragrant steam bathe her face. She studied her husband while he spooned the casserole into two bowls then sliced an apple, arranged the slices on a plate, and scooped a dollop on peanut butter in the middle. He was the most patient and loving man she'd ever known.

"I love you, Charles."

The smile that melted her heart so many years ago brightened his face.

"What are you smiling about?" She asked, and smiled back at him.

"I'm savoring the moment—here with you in our home. I love you too, Danielle Driscoll. I'm proud to call you my wife." He tenderly squeezed her hand across the table.

She raised her eyebrows. "Danielle? Are we getting serious now? Okay then seriously, what do you think of my idea?"

"I think you need to think about it a little longer."

"But, I have thought..."

"Shhhhh." He held a finger to his lips. "I'm not finished. I spoke with your friend Amanda this morning before I picked you up from the hospital. She saw your little appearance on the news and called to find out how you are. She's anxious to show you the mountain cabin she just bought."

"You want me to go to Amanda's? Now?"

"I think it's perfect timing. You obviously have a lot to think about, and a little distance might give you some perspective. And don't forget; Terrell has a suspect in custody for the Jennings robbery and murder, but according to you, it's not the man who kidnapped you. I think putting a little distance between you, and this city, could ensure your safety. At least until Terrell can get this worked out."

"You think Amanda will talk me out of this, don't you?" It was more of a statement than a question.

"It should be obvious that I haven't discussed your idea with Amanda, since you just brought it up."

"What I really want is your opinion, Charles. How do

you feel about the idea of being married to an investigative reporter?"

"To be honest, I don't know how I feel about it. I need some time to consider what that means to us–to your safety." He splayed his hands out on the table. "Why don't you take a week or two off, visit Amanda, and whatever you've decided when you get back, I'll support."

She grinned, carefully pushed herself up from the table, and hugged him with one arm. "Thank you Charles; that sounds like a good plan. I'll call Amanda tomorrow, and make arrangements. Tonight, all I want to do is snuggle up with you on the sofa, relax, and let the TV entertain us until we fall asleep."

Charles helped her into clean pajamas, and winced when he saw her bruised body. "Are you sure you don't want a pain pill?"

"No, I don't want one. I probably look worse than I feel. I'm sore but not really in pain." She slipped her cast into the sling.

"Okay. Let's get you downstairs, and settled on the sofa. I'll make hot chocolate."

Charles made her comfortable with pillows and a quilt, and handed her the remote. "Here you go, the remote's all yours tonight. I'll get some snacks while you channel surf."

Dani flipped through the available programming. None

of the movies sounded interesting, and she settled on one of the late night talk shows that she hardly ever stayed up long enough to watch.

"What are we watching?" Charles returned with steaming hot chocolate and a plate of graham crackers.

"A late night talk show. The host is funny."

Dani put her feet across Charles's lap, listening to the banter between the first guest, and the host. Her eyelids became heavy as the ebb and flow of emotions lulled her.

Peaceful, her breathing slowed, her head fell back against the arm of the sofa. She gave in, dozing in the serenity of being safe at home with her husband.

"Please welcome our next guests, who together hope to..."

She pulled the blanket tighter around her, dozing peacefully.

"That's not what I said. Now listen carefully."

Dani's eyes opened with a start. "Was I dreaming?"

"You were dozing. Want a sip of your hot chocolate to wake you up?" Charles offered her the cup.

"We are determined to eradicate breast cancer." The unmistakable voice yanked her from sleep, and reverberated in her head. Startling words—spoken in exactly the same way.

She stared toward the TV, pulled into consciousness by a face on the screen that she'd struggled so hard to see in the darkness of a few nights before. Her heart raced, beating so loud in her ears she had to struggle to hear the conversation.

"That's him!" She cried out, holding her hand to her heart. She felt as if there wasn't enough oxygen in the room, and she gasped.

"Sweetheart, you were dreaming. The psychologist thought you might have panic attacks. She said it was natural to re-live the events, or have trouble sleeping." He rubbed her feet and ankles.

She trembled, riveted to the television, and the man who looked vaguely familiar. The audience laughed and applauded. The camera zoomed out to reveal the second guest.

"Let's have a round of applause for Mona Davenport, Founder and CEO of The American Pink Ribbon Foundation, and Mr. Todd Hastings, VP of Sales at Diaxler Pharmaceuticals."

Dani pointed to the screen. "Charles, that man was at the hospital the day Dr. Jennings died. He was reading a newspaper in the waiting room, and he left as soon as Mrs. Jennings and her daughters came out of ICU. I didn't think anything about it at the time. I thought he looked familiar when I saw the video of Mona's big press release, but I couldn't quite place him."

She struggled to sit up. "That's the man who kidnapped me. I'm sure of it. Get me paper and a pen, I need to write down his name."

Charles shuffled through the coffee table drawer and handed her a tablet. "I'm calling Terrell," he said.

# CHAPTER 46

Terrell paced back and forth in front of the wall of windows overlooking the tarmac at Denver International Airport. "The plane is late." He checked his watch again.

"The board says it just landed; we should see it any minute." Collins said.

"And you're sure this is the right flight?" Terrell couldn't remember being this nervous about apprehending a suspect.

"Holt, for the tenth time, yes I confirmed it. Just chill for ten more minutes. They're both in first class. Hastings should be one of the first off the plane. We'll get him." Collins swallowed the rest of her coffee, and tossed the cup in the recycle bin.

Passengers began to file into the arrival gate, and Terrell spotted his suspect about six people back. As soon as he stepped clear of the crowd, Terrell was on him.

"Todd Hastings?"

"That's right." The muscles in Todd's jaw rippled.

"Step aside, please." Terrell led Todd toward the windows and left Collins to wait for Mona.

Terrell closed handcuffs over this suspect's wrists. "Todd Hastings, you're under arrest for the kidnapping, and attempted murder of Danielle Driscoll."

"My goodness." Mona's shrill voice carried across several gates, alerting the other passengers, who turned and stared. "Whatever is going on? Todd?"

"Mona Davenport?" Collins asked.

Mona swallowed hard, looking at the growing number of onlookers, her face contorted with unspoken confusion. "Yes, of course dear. I'm Mona Davenport; everyone knows that."

"Right. Ms. Davenport, we need you for questioning. You can either ride with us to the station, or meet us there in an hour." She tapped the address on her business card, and handed it to Mona.

"My dear, what could you possibly..."

Collins apparently had no patience for dramatics. "Ms. Davenport, can I trust you to meet me at the station in an hour, or do I need to haul you in, too?"

Mona snatched the card, pursed her lips, and adjusted the designer shoulder bag she was carrying. "Of course, you can trust me, I'm CEO of the biggest..."

"Save it." Collins looked at her watch, "One hour."

Terrell nodded to Collins and the two of them led Todd through the airport, ignoring the clamor of reporters who shouted questions, and followed the handcuffed suspect through the airport.

"Mr. Hastings, did you kidnap Dani Driscoll?"

"Detective Holt! Does Dani Driscoll know there's been an arrest in her kidnapping?"

"Mr. Hastings, were you responsible for the Tribune reporter who firemen rescued from a burning building?"

"Mr. Hastings! Mr. Hastings! What was your motive?"

Dani stood in front of the small, brightly lit room, and watched six men wearing orange jump suits file in, and face her. Her eyes fixed on the man who terrorized her, and left her to burn to death. He was standing right in front of her, separated only by a sheet of glass. She shivered. There was no mistaking him. She closed her fingers tighter around Charles's hand, even though she knew the men in the line-up couldn't see her.

"Number five. That's the man I saw at the hospital the night Dr. Jennings died. I'm sure of it, Terrell."

Terrell nodded, and took the microphone. "Gentleman, when I call your number, step forward and repeat these words exactly. *Listen carefully and I'll tell you exactly what I want.*"

327

When number five took his turn repeating the words, she identified him again. "It's number five. He's trying to disguise his voice, but I'll never forget it. He's the man who kidnapped me."

"Thank you, Dani. We'll ask the judge to refuse bail for your protection. This case is as iron-clad as they come, thanks to you."

Her lips quivered, and she pushed through the tears that threatened to flow. "Terrell, I don't know how to thank you." Her breath hitched.

"Come on, let's get you some fresh air." Terrell lead them out through the side door.

"And Mona?" Dani asked.

"Strictly off the record. I interrogated her myself, and she'll have to testify when this goes to court. But I don't believe she was involved in your kidnapping, or in the Jennings murder. It was Hastings who hired Snipes to eliminate Dr. Jennings. It seems all Mona is guilty of is greed."

"Hastings confessed then?"

"No, but Snipes did when I told him we had Hastings in custody. He was terrified, and made a deal to be held in a different facility than Hastings, even after they're both sentenced."

"Then it all boiled down to money." Dani shook her head. "If only Mona's supporters knew how she manipulates the truth. Selling hope in the name of a cure when the best hope we have is still sitting in the Jennings lab, yet unfunded."


The End

I hope you enjoyed reading Hope, Inc. as much as I loved writing it.

Dani Driscoll has many more investigations in her future. Her next adventure will put her at the scene of an earthquake with her friend, Amanda.

*Fracture*, Volume Two in the Dani Driscoll Series is coming soon.

LoucindaSullivan.com